20th Anniversary Edition

I0571123

A Street Called

Pain

BY

B. BENEDICT BRADDOCK

A Street Called Pain

20th Anniversary Edition

B. Benedict Braddock

Empathy Books

Humanservicesconsultants@gmail.com

" *The World breaks everyone, and afterward many are strong at the broken places.*"

- Ernest Hemingway

Table of Contents

Foreword

The events portrayed in this story occur at a time when the United States government (as it later did with the Katrina catastrophe) became not only an active witness, but a faceless co-conspirator of the ever emerging popularity of crack cocaine. America's war on drugs was and still is a monster like masquerade designed to hide its complicitous participation in the genocide of millions of its citizens as well as the multi-billion dollar profiteering amongst nefarious beneficiaries. Be it a top draft choice college basketball star who died from crack cocaine before he even played his first game, a pro-football star whose autopsy shows cocaine in his system; the participation of elected civil-servants, unethical members of the national/international financial communities, exploitable mules and most disturbingly, the victimization of our children (born and unborn) this was by far one of the most horrific massacres of the human condition in American history.

B. Benedict Braddock or "B" as he is known to his family and friends has authored numerous books, short stories and original screenplays. In "A Street Called Pain" Braddock has crafted a bird's eye view of the ravaging effects of addiction and spiritual chaos on the three main characters, Benny, Star and Cole. They, along with fellow addicts Joe, Junior and Con, wage a fatalistic war to recapture that "never as good as the first time" high. It will forever elude them but that's a non-concern. In the meantime however there is the "mission". Yes the ever loveless call to healing dishonor and desolation--- "Missioning." If anything, missioning was often far more dangerous than the actual sought after poison, but when an addict is sick for what they need they just need it. It doesn't matter what it is or what it takes to get it.

While addiction is the mainstay of this macabre

meditation on human nihilism, there are the surprises. Some of them good, some of them bad. We are reminded that while the narcotic poisoned mind can be a dangerously altered mind it is not always completely void of invaluable insight lacking amongst many so called healthy, addiction free Americans. This is something we become aware of through the ruminations which take place in Benny's subconscious. "A Street Called Pain" is not just a place in any big city, rural community or small town, but a place that can exist inside of you. Where do you go when the world appears to no longer have a place for you, but you're not yet ready to die? If we learn nothing else we learn that addiction is a disease. It is a disease which at its most pervasive can bring the worst out of all of us...particularly those who are not personally suffering from addiction.

--Actor Tomas Boykin

Chapter One: The Beginning

Have you ever called anyone a nigger? Any idea what that meant or if you meant it at all? What about calling a female a hoe or a skank or a bitch? How must it feel to be on the receiving end of these words? What's it like to be poor? To be broken down and used up? What about the addicts? Do they even deserve to be considered? Do they have feelings like everybody else?

I have, on occasion, jumped rope with little black girls in the ghetto. I've sat and listened to the stories of old men on the front stoops of some of the nastiest streets you can imagine. I've helped a single mother carry hard earned groceries into a filthy, rat-infested apartment building. These are the innocents, the heroes, the role models. I know them all. And the addicts? I know them best.

The ghetto is the ghetto no matter where you go. Ghetto, project, planned neighborhood, bad area. It's all the same be it in New York, Chicago, Philly, Detroit, Miami, wherever. The same sights and sounds assault you and your senses are on constant alert for trouble of any kind. There are the dealers and the addicted, the working girls and the johns, the thieves and the victimized, the runaways and those searching for them. There are cops and bad guys and sometimes they are one in the same. But always you see the sunken faces and desperation of lives that were doomed from the start. Souls trapped inside of walking skeletons.

I'm sitting here on the front stoop of Cole's house smoking a cigarette and watching Demond deal vials of crack down the block. Rita's searching around by his feet looking for any small pieces he might have dropped. Demond and two other men are making fun of her and Demond keeps slapping her ass and howling like an idiot. She doesn't even seem to notice. She's too bugged out. She slowly makes her way up toward me and tries to entice me by hiking her skirt up over bruised and dirty thighs. I go to her, all the while keeping my eye on Demond and hand her five bucks.

"Get outta the street Rita before someone runs you over."

Rita tries her best to smile. She tries to speak but can't. She takes the bill and runs clumsily back to Demond who hands her a vial and laughs. He looks up the hill at me and our eyes lock. I mouth the words "fuck you". He smiles and goes about his business.

I used to like to party. But in truth it was deeper than that. I was bored with my life. With the same thing everyday bullshit that most people do for their entire fucking lives. I was bored with my job, with the people I knew, with my car, my clothes, my watch, my socks, the whole boring fuckin' ordeal. So I got into a little coke and some cocktails. I started banging the bad girl bar whores and showing up for work wearing the same suit I'd left in at five o'clock the previous day. The more I dove into the darkness the more bored I got with the sunlight. Pretty soon the job was gone and with it the parties on the veranda. I isolated myself and coked up alone. It was never enough anyway. I knew I needed something more and I set out to find it. The day I made that decision is the day I met Cole. Terrence Coleman, though he'll kill you if you call him that. Most people just called him Doc. He always had their medicine. No insurance accepted.

I myself didn't live in the ghetto then. I lived the common suburban life of a young white male with a job. I had a small but nice studio and all of the toys people seemed to want but it just wasn't doing much for me. I drove the ten miles to the "rough side of town" and began to search for someone who could do better than the shit I was buying in the bar which was cut so badly with baking soda you could taste the crap in your throat.

This part of town was certainly in disrepair. Row houses and old brick apartment buildings, most of which were low income projects, lined the pot-holed streets. Most of the old phone booths were cracked and damaged and most of the pay phones without a receiver. There were plenty of liquor stores and check cashing places, discount stores with faded old signs, sneakers hanging over electrical lines and plenty of rough looking people. I cruised around looking for just the right guy who could supply what I was looking for.

I pulled my candy apple red corvette around the corner and spotted him instantly. He was in his mid to late thirties, very dark skinned, and about six feet tall. He was a sight to behold with his mangled hair, outdated three dollar shades, white painter's pants stained with various colors of paint, and an out of fashion striped shirt. To complete the look he wore a baby blue sport jacket a few sizes too big which one could smartly assume concealed a weapon. He was just completing a transaction as I pulled to the curb and I signaled to him. He looked into the car at me, smirked, then turned and started to walk away.

I climbed out and followed him for a moment.

"Got nuthin to say to the fuckin Five-O," he said over his shoulder.

I pretended to ignore him while I searched in my pocket for the folded piece of aluminum foil that contained my blow. I opened it, scooped a little up with my fingernail, and snorted a blast right there on the street. Cole jumped back and glanced around for onlookers. He looked spooked at first but then let out a wild laugh.

"Ha! Nigga cops do that shit like that all the time. This ain't no dumb ass street nigga you gonna trap wit' some dumb ass shit like that."

I reached out my hand to him. "Name's Benny."

Cole just looked at me like a roach he needed to step on. His smirk told me he planned to enjoy it.

"Shit." He spat on the sidewalk and turned to walk away again.

"I've got five hundred on me," I called after him.

"Now I knows you Five-O. Ain't nobody out here wit' that kinda bread man."

"Alright," I said. "Fuck you."

I turned to walk away and he watched a moment before calling out to me.

"Cops ain't allowed to say they ain't cops and then bust your ass man."

"First of all," I laughed, "that's some street corner bullshit that people believe but it's not true. Second, I'm not a cop. If you want to make some money let's go or else I'm leaving."

We stopped and looked at each other for a long moment, sizing each other up.

Cole sniffed. "Where you from man?"

"Other side of the tracks."

"Hear dat."

Talking to Cole was like talking to an old black man in front of the barber shop. He would ponder every word I said before answering me. He'd rub his chin in thought constantly and raise his eyebrows when he was amused. He'd mumbled, Mmmm Hmmm, as I spoke. He became in a way a mentor for me on the street. He looked out for me.

Cole would ramble on for hours weaving masterful tales like a gifted storyteller.

"So this man comes back outta his house and walks over to me wit' this shit eatin' smile. He hands me, listen ta dis shit, fifty dollah's."

"Get outta her," I smile.

"HA! Fifty fuckin' dollars man! So I look the man up an' down an' he smilin' and shit like he done me a favor an' shit ya know? And I say to the man, I been paintin' on your house for two fuckin' days an' you hand me this shit right here. I'll put this shit here right the fuck up your ass boy. Go get your sorry butt up in your house an' get me my money."

By now of course others in the bar had drawn closer to listen to Cole's animated tale.

"So what'd he say?" I asked.

Cole sipped his beer. "He said no."

"So what'd you do?"

"I kicked his sorry ass up an' down the street for all his cracker ass neighbors to see. Then I went to six months in the county jail."

I smiled. "So was it worth it?"

Cole rubbed his chin in thought for a moment. "Fuck yeah."

The bar exploded in laughter and conversation. Cole had a way of relaxing people. He was simply not a fast track kind of guy. He'd sit with you all day sipping cheap beer and smoking even cheaper cigarettes. "These taste like shit," he'd say before immediately lighting another. He turned to look at me and raised his chin.

"So, what about you?"

"Oh, nothing. I got stopped for speeding and had half a gram on me. I got thirty days for a first violation and a year's probation."

Cole smirked at me. "Half a gram. I think I got that much spilled on my sleeve right now."

"Did I mention I was also drunk?"

"Naw. You neglected to say."

We smiled into our mugs for a moment, enjoying the quiet joke before Cole was off again with another story to entertain the bar. You didn't need a juke box with Cole around.

Trust developed quickly between us. We got together a lot over the next couple of months just drinking and fucking with the girls on the street. We hit the pipe in more than one tavern and got thrown out on our asses just as many times. We accepted each other for what we were, different, yet still the same.

———————————•◆◆•———————————

Cole's house was furnished with thirty year old easy

chairs and an ugly brown couch that even the Salvation Army wouldn't take. Some five and dime paintings hung here and there on the walls which were badly cracked and faded. The carpet looked like it had never been cleaned and the whole place reeked of cigarette smoke.

The old house sat on a hill at the very top of a dead end street. Behind it was wooded with the highway just beyond the trees. You could see parts of the city down below and Cole reigned over the neighborhood from the house as if he were a king sitting up high upon his mountain. As far as security was concerned the house could not be better situated. You could easily run up the back trail to the highway and be gone in minutes. You could see who was approaching long before they reached the house. Best of all, were the police to come down on the block, they wouldn't come undetected.

We were bored. Cole sat slouched in his chair watching a cockroach climb up his beer bottle. He flicked it away as it neared the top. I sat on the sofa, intently watching my cigarette slowly burn. I was trying to burn the whole thing without any of the ashes falling off to the floor. The screen door suddenly swung open with a loud bang and my ashes fell as I twitched.

In the door came three dark skinned men about Cole's age. Two of them were thuggish looking types and the third wore a shirt and tie. They stopped short in their tracks when they saw me and Cole stumbled up out of his chair grinning from ear to ear. He swung his open palms out toward me as if presenting a painting at auction.

"Dis here my boy B."

He pointed out each of the other men. "Dat Junior, Dat Con, and Dat pussy ass lil' nigga is Joe."

"Fuck you man," Joe countered.

The three men let their guard down, quite obviously relieved. Junior nodded to me. "What up B?"

Con smirked. "Thought for a minute you was the parole man. My ass shouldn't be here man.

We sat and passed a cheap bottle of vodka around for

about an hour talking about anything and nothing. I lit up another smoke and passed around what was left of my pack. Junior commented on needing something stronger. I fully agreed. Junior turned to Cole who rolled his head as if with great effort to meet Junior's gaze.

"No cash, blood."

"I have some."

They all turned to me. "I do."

Before they could respond the screen door banged open again and two more thuggish looking men entered. They were both black, one about my age in his mid-twenties and the other maybe thirty-five or so. They were dressed entirely in black and wore combat boots. They stopped short just as the others had, staring first at me and then at Cole. The older of the two men spoke first.

"What's a white boy doin' up in here?"

Cole looked around as if it were news to him. His gaze swept past me, then the rest of the guys, then back to me. "You talkin' 'bout B?"

Junior, Con and Joe laughed. They got Cole laughing. "Nigga ain't white, nigga jus' light."

They continued to laugh until Cole noticed that the other man had me fixed in a fierce glare. He stopped laughing and his expression turned uncomfortably dark.

"You'll leave here in a bag first cuz."

The man shot me one last look before turning to his younger companion. "Where the bitch at?"

The younger man retreated outside and came right back in pulling a young Hispanic woman along behind him. The three swept past us and into the kitchen. Cole smiled at me.

"Jus' my dumb ass cousin Demond comin' round to play out the country nigga's and steal my business."

Cole stood to stretch his back. "How much we gettin' B?"

I checked my pocket. "I got a hundred on me. I'll go and meet you back."

Cole pointed up with his thumb. "Attic."

I exited through the front and Cole and the others passed the bottle around again. Cole sat down across from Junior and nodded to him.

"Where you been?"

"Out tryin' to find something."

"You can't find your dick wit' out me."

"You think about my dick a lot huh?"

"You lucky I'm tired cuz."

"Tired and sad."

"That's alright man you go ahead. I ain't mad at ya. I'll catch up wit' your sorry ass later."

Junior laughed. " No worries bro."

Cole flicked a bottle cap at him. "Hear it but don't believe it."

"So you know this B?"

"Yeah, he cool."

"You sure man? You say it I'm cool. It's jus' I been hearin' shit about the five-O and judges an' shit hittin' the pipe."

"Ain't no crackhead judges man."

"Maybe cops though?"

"Ain't no crackhead cops."

"How you know?

"Man, the cops is drinkin' peppermint schnapps an' shit. They ain't down with no mutha fuckin' rocks. I swear you listen to the dumbest ass niggas you can find jus' to bring this shit home to me."

Junior slouched down a bit in his seat. "Some people might know is all."

"Some people might be freakin' on a bad load man."

"Shit man, you don't know."

"If I don't know then why you ask me? Shut your punk ass up."

The screen door slammed again and a very pretty young black woman entered with a bang. Star came in on them like a hurricane, shouting, "What's up, What's up!" like she was rousing a concert crowd. Cole grabbed his chest feigning a heart attack.

"Woman, must you come up in here like that every day? Sometimes ten times a day. Sometimes twenty times a day."

Star ignored him. She quickly paced the room checking everything out. She walked to the kitchen doorway, peeked in, and scrunched up her nose at what she saw. She came back to the center of the living room and stopped short to look at herself in the mirror. She began to parade in front of the men, acting out modeling poses and spinning around with her arms out wide. The men ignored her and sipped their beer and vodka. Star raised her hand up high.

"Tell me I don't look good."

Cole looked up. "You don't look good."

"Why you lyin'?"

She looked over her shoulder at her rear.

"Tell me my ass don't look good in these pants."

Cole grumbled. "Your ass wouldn't look good on Janet Jackson."

The others laughed.

"Yeah, yeah," she shot back. "You laughin' cause you know you can't get none."

Cole sighed at her. "You just a baby."

"Yeah a baby doll. Make your dumb ass drool."

"Shit," Cole mumbled.

Start sat down on the arm of Cole's chair.

"Finally girl, damn."

She grabbed his beer and took a deep swig. "So tell me what up?"

"My boy out gettin' us some."

"Who your boy?"

"B."

"Don't know no B. 'Cept that crazy ass brother come round last year fuckin' wit' y'all. Ain't seen his ass since. He dead?"

Con smirked. "We wouldn't know."

"I ever seen this nigga before Doc?" she asked.

"Cole smiled. "Don't think so. And don't scare the man away neither."

"You just tell him I ain't no hoochie."

Cole stood up. "I cannot tell a lie. Come on, let's go up. I don't wanna be down here when Demond's shit start."

The attic was the safe place. Four floors up with a triple deadlocked hollow steel door and drop bar. The police or would- be thieves looking to steal Cole's stash would need to drive to the top of the hill, rush the front door, climb three levels of stairs, break down the reinforced door, and climb another flight of stairs to get to us. Cole had decided that it would be nearly impossible to do all of that and find any evidence left by the time they reached the attic. The space wasn't large. The slanted roof made it necessary to crouch as you walked. There was a full size bed, two easy chairs, and four metal folding chairs. A single small window looked out upon an alley between the houses with a fairly decent view of any traffic that might be coming up the hill as well.

While the others made their way up to the sanctuary, I set out to complete the business they were waiting on. I found Rita and some fairly decent looking other chick just after I'd made my purchase. They were both trembling slightly and looking to cop some rock. I'd just placed a small bag in Rita's hand and she looked pissed.

"These ain't no twenties."

"Nope. They're dimes."

"Then why you tell us twenty?"

"Did I just walk a half an hour just to come back here and hand it to you with no profit?"

Rita smiled and looked me up and down a moment. She slid her hand down to her thigh and lifted her skirt slightly as she flicked her tongue.

"How 'bout we take care of each baby? The three of us?"

I was all for that. I walked over to the pay phone and dialed Cole's number. He answered as he always did. "Who is it?"

He listened for a minute, rubbing his chin and mumbling, " Mmm, Hmm".

He smiled and said, "Be right there."

Cole hung up the phone and nearly knocked Star over as he headed for the steps.

She spilled her beer on her pants and was pissed.

"What the fuck man!"

Cole blew her a kiss. "Back in a flash."

I couldn't help but smile at the rather cartoon- like way Cole came running down the hill with a huge grin on his face. He stopped short and looked over the girls.

"Give 'em half."

"I handed over the bags to the girls and Cole grabbed Rita's friend by the hand.

"This one's mine."

Cole took off in a jog down behind a convenience store, dragging the girl along behind him. Rita took me by the hand and led me into the alley.

"You and I are going to become real good friends," she said as she knelt down in front of me.

"I smiled down at her. "God I sure hope so."

Cole climbed back up the steps to the attic looking exhausted. Star glared at him ferociously. "Where you been? We been waitin' for half an hour! Where's your boy?"

"He comin'," Cole smiled. "Believe me he comin'."

Demond and his boy had taken over the living room by the time I got back. The young Hispanic girl was naked and bent over the side of an easy chair with her head resting on the seat. She was noticeably wasted and her eyes were wild and darting about. She was still clearly straight enough to be humiliated which I was certain was the point.

"Can I go now?" she asked.

Demond scowled at her. "You made the deal bitch. You smoked all night and you assume the position all day."

He walked up behind her and unzipped his pants. He looked at me and grinned a dark grin. I turned and headed up the steps.

Cole was sitting back on the bed, wiping his forehead with a dirty rag. The other three guys were seated about the room.

"We got a sixth man," Cole said. "She in the bathroom."

"She?"

Before he could answer, Star came bounding up the steps, talking loudly as she came.

"Here I come, here I come...time for the meetin'...sorry I'm late but I..."

Star reached the top of the steps, saw me, stopped short and shut up. Our eyes locked for a moment and hers got very wide. I raised my eyebrow and she walked over very quickly to sit beside Cole. I followed her with my eyes, unable to stop staring at her. She nudged Cole with her elbow. He turned to look at her. "What?"

Star just glared at him.

"Oh, yeah. This here is Star. She one of the brutha's. Don't suck no dick for hits yo."

I smiled. "You don't look like a brother."

Star looked me up and down. "You neither, pale ass cracker."

Cole nodded at me. "This here my boy B."

She snorted a little. "Just like that huh?"

"Yeah," Cole nodded. "Jus' like that."

She lifted her hands as if in surrender. "Alright, cool."

I took my seat and began to pass out bags to the men. Star was beautiful. She looked like a gang banger dressed in baggy purple jeans and a white flannel shirt that Cole could've wrapped around him twice. But she was beautiful. She had light skin, long curly hair, and wore wire rimmed glasses that made her look a bit nerdy. The moment I saw her I wanted her. I got up to hand her a bag and Cole smiled to himself.

"Oh you a charmer? Those arms ain't never seen no sun. You the whitest white-boy I ever seen."

Junior, Con and Joe laughed. Cole gave her a hard stare.

"I told you hoe, this is my boy."

"I ain't scared a you and I ain't no hoe you crack smokin', malt liquor suckin', broom pushin' nigga."

The men all laughed and Cole ruffled Star's hair.

"Star here an educated bitch. Better'n the other bitches cause she finished the High School."

"With honors," she added. "And proud of it."

Cole and Star joined in unison. "I am black, and proud, I stand tall, and proud…"

"'Nough a that shit," Cole handed me a pipe. "Try this here, B."

Cole handed me a glass crack pipe and I held a lighter to the end, being very careful not to spill the precious contents. I took the hit and closed my eyes. The others watched silently as I felt the rush come over me and my head got very light. When I opened my eyes again I knew they were wild and bugged out.

"Aww shit now," Star said. "That lil' white dick gonna get hard and the new nigga'll be chasin' my fine ass all over the house."

The others broke into laughter.

"You oughta give him some," Cole answered. "Bout

29

time you got a man worth somethin'."

"This boy ain't never had a sister man. He'd be cryin' an' shit if I worked his ass over."

Junior took a hit with his own pipe. He got to his feet with bugged out eyes, unblinking, and walked to the top of the stairs. He just stood there, looking down, motionless. Cole smiled and called out to him. "Anybody comin?"

"No," he replied evenly.

Con and Joe took their hits and followed up with a slug of vodka. Cole and Star followed suit. There was a heavy silence in the room and everyone wore frightened and paranoid expressions. Suddenly a loud knock sounded at the lower door and Junior nearly jumped out of his own skin. He made his way clumsily over to Cole and motioned toward the staircase as if Cole hadn't heard. Cole shouted down.

"Who dat?"

A voice called back from downstairs. "Doc, some white

boys out here wanna cop man."

Cole shrugged. "I ain't invited no white boys up here," he shouted back.

The voice persisted. "They got the President's man. Heavy."

Junior stood back up, pulled a gun from behind his back, and headed for the steps with a fierce look. Cole jumped up and grabbed him from behind, steering him back into his seat. He took the gun from Junior and tucked it beneath his shirt. "Sounds like a job for the Doc and B."

Four college age white guys, dressed like preppies, were leaning against a pricey SUV right in front of Cole's house. They stuck out in the neighborhood like a sore thumb and were already drawing attention. Cole and I came out the door and the screen banged loudly, startling one of the boys who had been daydreaming. Cole walked up within ten feet of them and stopped.

"What up?"

One of them stepped forward. "Someone told us we could score here."

Cole rubbed his chin. "Score?"

The man nodded. "Yes."

"Cool. I'll turn 'round and drop my drawls and you boys come get it while it's hot."

I burst out laughing and got Cole laughing. The young guy laughed along nervously. "Seriously though, we'd like to buy some coke."

"Ohhh," Cole exaggerated. "You wanna buy some coke."

"Yes," he nodded.

"Paper or plastic?"

Cole couldn't even get the words out before he and I were laughing hysterically. You know how sometimes you get laughing so hard that you can't stop and can't seem to get any words out? The white boys simply stood there and watched us, unsure what to do or not to do. They knew Cole was messing with them.

"Listen y'all," Cole finally said. "I don't even know who you are but you jus' drive up to the first brutha you see an' ask to buy drugs? Come on now."

"No, no." another of the men stepped forward. "It's not like that at all. I have a lot of friends who are black. We're cool. It's okay."

I started to feel a bit sorry for them. "Aww hell, give 'em a break Doc."

Cole looked them up and down a bit as if he was deciding whether or not he could trust them. As soon as he spoke I knew what he was going to do.

"You have a lot of friends who are black?"

"Yeah man," the guy replied.

Cole sighed. "Fine, Gimme the money."

The two guys each handed Cole some cash which he counted out to one hundred dollars. "Guess what," he smiled. "You ain't got no black friends here. Later y'all."

He turned back toward the house with a wide grin. The two boys stepped forward as if to grab him and Cole turned back on them with a menacing look. He pulled up the tail of his shirt to reveal the pistol tucked into his waistband and tapped the grip with his fingernails.

"Play time over boys. Tell your Moms and Pops I said Hi. Tell your Moms sorry i ain't been 'round in a while. Too many hoe's a my own to deal wit."

The men stared at Cole with obvious anger. He could tell that they were thinking of rushing him and he tilted his head slightly to the side and studied them. "Don't you boys wanna have a happy future?"

They turned to me and I just shrugged. I hadn't even known what Cole was planning when we came down. They turned and walked back to their vehicle, backed down the hill slowly, turned and peeled away with a screech. Cole stared down the hill. "Dumb ass white boys."

"Easy now man," I smiled. "It's just business."

Cole counted out half of the money and handed it to me. "That's all it is man."

We climbed back up the steps to the sound of loud hip-hop music. Star was dancing with her thumb hooked in the front of her pants, swinging her hips wildly. They guys were lounging and ignoring her as usual. We stopped and watched her for a moment, Cole standing just behind me.

"Girl crazy man."

I smiled. " I like that kind of crazy."

"I see you do."

"Think she'll go for a white guy?"

"Don't matter. I don't know no white guy."

We laughed and Star stopped dancing for a second.

"I know you talkin' 'bout me."

"Your head as big as your ass," Cole answered.

"Yeah, tell me my ass ain't all that."

Cole snorted. "Your ass all that plus a lil' extra just in case."

"I dunno man," I smiled again. "I think her ass looks

pretty good."

Star had the very faintest of a smile as she placed her hands on her hips. "You dunno? You know damn well boyfriend."

We all took our seats as we had been before and Cole produced a small screwdriver to scrape down the resin inside his pipe into the filter. He took a deep hit. Star began to dance again and I couldn't seem to keep my eyes off of her. She saw me watching and turned away quickly, a real smile on her face this time.

It was dark outside with only a couple working lights on a few scattered houses to illuminate the street. Cole and I sat on the curb in front of his house passing a bottle of malt liquor back and forth and surveying the neighborhood. I lit two smokes and handed one to him. "Quiet here at night."

"Is tonight," he nodded and glanced around. "Come 'round first a the month. Shit be like grand central. Crackheads out like roaches wit' them state checks."

"You make money then?"

"Make it and smoke it man. Broke the next day like everybody else."

"We need a system."

"A system? Boy you don't need no system. You need a mutha fuckin' gun. The hardware is the system."

"No man. You gotta use your head to work, not your back."

"Ha! First time a white man ever said that to me."

"What I'm saying is, I still have a little cash in the bank. If we do this right, and carefully, we'll never go broke."

Cole sat and rubbed his chin in quiet thought for a few moments. "So, what you think of Star?"

"She makes me a little nervous, but at the same time I'm a little intrigued."

"You should be nervous. Don't mind me sayin' but you ain't used to her kind. But she cool man. I make sure she alright."

"That sounds just a little bit like a warning. I'm not stepping on your toes am I?"

"It ain't like that. Jus' come with respect is all I'm sayin'."

"I'm a little surprised you do the big brother thing. It doesn't seem to be your style."

"Then you ain't been payin' attention."

Across the street a front door opened and a little Puerto Rican girl about seven came out clutching some money in her hand. She headed down the street toward the convenience store on the corner. Out of nowhere a rail-thin black man came from the darkness and snatched her money from her. She yelled out in a heavy accent. "Heeeey! What you doin'?"

The man shoved her away and pocketed the money.

Cole was up and running full speed toward the man who never saw him until it was too late. Cole smashed the liquor bottle over the man's head and he went down hard to the ground. Cole took the money back out of the man's pocket and handed it back to the little girl. She nodded her head as if she'd just received justice.

"Hurry up now," Cole told her. "Your Mama gonna beat your ass for takin' so long."

The girl turned to run into the store. "Thank you Mistah Cole!"

Cole walked back up the hill to me and I held up the empty bottle we'd finished earlier. "You had to use the full one?"

Cole smirked. "What man?"

"The empty one wouldn't have dropped him?"

"Ha! You sicker'n me mutha fucka."

Cole sat down beside me to catch his breath and I turned to face him. "You know what's bothering me?"

"What's that?"

"That shit your cousin's putting that girl through in the house. All day man. It's too much."

Cole nodded. "Yeah. Nough's a nough."

We burst in quickly to Cole's living room startling Demond and his boy. The girl was lying naked on the floor face down and the two men were sitting in arm chairs looking high and nervous. I headed straight for Demond while Cole wrapped a chain around the other man's neck and yanked him up over the back of his chair. Demond tried to run but I grabbed him by the back of his head and shoved him down till his face hit the floor. He rolled over to fight but found the gun right in his face and froze. He opened his arms wide to let me know he wasn't going to move.

"You two crackheads dumb enough to try an' rob me?" He snickered.

I pressed the gun to his lips. "Open up and suck it."

"Fuck you bitch."

I shoved the gun forcefully into Demond's mouth and pushed it in and out as he squirmed. "Now tell the girl she's free to go."

"All this over some hoe?" he laughed.

"Tell her," I demanded.

"Fine. Your funeral man. Day almost over anyway. Go on bitch, get out."

The girl gathered up her clothes and ran out the front door naked. I got up and slowly backed away from him. Cole shoved the other guy toward the door, kicked him in the ass, and threw him out.

"Now get the fuck out," I said to Demond.

He got up slowly, smiled, calmly tucked in his shirt, and walked toward the front door. He stopped and winked at Cole. "I'll see you real soon cuz. You know it."

Cole held his glare. "Don't come back."

The screen door slammed behind the men and Cole and I collapsed on the sofa. Cole closed his eyes for a moment to calm himself.

"This is what I'm talkin' about," I said. "Keep everybody else outta here. We'll sell the shit ourselves."

Cole nodded. "We outta beer B."

"We smoked up all the money already."

"Now what?"

We must have looked like we were out of our minds as we burst back outside into Cole's front yard. We certainly felt half crazed as we jogged down the hill with Cole's chain dangling from his hand. A young thug-looking guy passed by on a bicycle and Cole whipped the chain at him, hitting him in the back. Cole tried to swing again to knock him off the bike but the man escaped just in time. "My fuckin' hood!" Cole screamed after him.

A second young guy came around the corner and ran straight into Cole who wrapped the chain around his neck and began to slap the shit out of him. Blood appeared from the man's nose and he looked scared stiff.

"I hope you got my money man," Cole growled.

"The man's voice was broken and trembling. ""I only got twenty Doc. I was just coming to see you."

"Give it here."

The man pulled out a twenty dollar bill and handed it over. Cole nodded for me to pat him down.

"What do we have here?" I asked. I pulled out a packet of aluminum foil and opened it up to find four decent size pieces of rock cocaine."

"Good," Cole spit at the man. "Now we don't feel bad."

Cole kneed the man hard in the groin and he went down howling in pain. He stood over him a moment and stared at him darkly. For a moment he actually scared me a bit. Then he simply turned and headed back up the hill, with me following and thinking only of the drugs.

Chapter Two: The Hook

My apartment was a clean, fairly good size studio, with polished hardwood floors, a bed, kitchenette, two recliners, an entertainment center, and a small table where I sat scraping down the precious cocaine residue in my glass pipe. The studio had a pretty view of the woods just beyond the building but these days I kept the blinds tightly closed and often checked to make very certain that no one could see in. This of course was pure paranoia since I was on the second floor and it was a straight drop down from the window with no possible access. A loud knock at the door startled me and I quickly hid the pipe behind a chair cushion and went to answer. I opened the door to the expressionless face of Star.

"I saw that you lived here."

"Come in."

She entered and looked around for a moment. "Nice. I need a shower."

I was a bit startled. "Uh, yeah sure. Right in there. Towels are in the closet."

"Thanks, here."

She handed me a bag of crack vials and a crude pipe made out of a pill bottle, a piece of a pen, and some rubber bands.

"Wait'll I get in and hook me up with a blast. Bring it in to me."

I nodded as Star walked into the bathroom and closed the door over. I started to prepare her pipe as requested but had only just opened one of the vials when she came back out wearing only a very tiny pair of panties, revealing an absolutely perfect body.

"You got a pair of boxers and a T-shirt I can borrow?"

"Uh, yeah," I stammered. "Right here."

I grabbed them from a dresser drawer and handed them to her.

"Thanks."

She turned and walked back into the bathroom and I stood with my eyes frozen on her ass until she closed over the door again. I put my hands over my face and slid them down slowly until they were in a praying position beneath my chin. I was incredibly excited and a bit off guard but I took a deep breath and went back to the task of preparing the pipe with shaky hands. When I heard the shower turn on I took the pipe, tapped on the bathroom door and entered. The curtain was closed and I debated for a moment on whether or not I should just pull it open. She had, after all, just walked into my house, got naked, and got into my shower. An engraved invitation wouldn't be necessary. I reached for the curtain but then pulled my hand back.

"Here you go."

"Hand it in to me."

Another dilemma I thought. Should I now pull open the curtain or just pass the pipe around to her. I reached around and immediately regretted not being bolder.

I heard Star. "Hmmm."

Was she amused by getting the pipe in the shower or reacting to my being such an incredible pussy and not yanking that damn curtain back? Was she wondering if maybe I wasn't interested or ready or God-forbid able, or was she simply having herself a good time with her drugs? She was making me uncomfortable yet still exciting me, taking the control of my own home away from me. She was brilliant.

Smoke came out from behind the curtain and Star placed the pipe on the corner of the tub where I could reach it without seeing her. I debated for another second. I should, I thought, just join her in the shower and nail her right now. That was clearly what she was inviting right? Or maybe I was just being foolish. The girl pretty much lived on the streets. It was very possible she just wanted a shower. I took the pipe and walked out, closing the door behind me.

Across town Cole was sitting on his bed in the dim light, loading a pipe with trembling hands. He took a hit, sat there a moment, started to gurgle, and vomited all over himself. He reached for another rock, loaded up the pipe, and hit it again. Vomit dripped from his chin as he took a mouthful of vodka, spit it out on the floor, then took another deep chug. He climbed back into the corner of his bed, pulled his knees up protectively, and began to tremble more violently. His eyes darted about the room and became wild and bugged out. He reacted to things unseen and unheard, reaching beneath his pillow for the revolver.

I was pacing about the room when Star emerged from the bathroom with wet hair and wearing my boxers and T-shirt. She clearly wasn't wearing a bra and my hopes were once again lifted. She looked incredibly sexy.

"You're next."

I hadn't been planning on taking a shower but I wasn't an idiot either. I tried to sound cool and collected. "Yeah, that sounds good right now."

I grabbed some underwear from a drawer and went on in to undress. I had just entered the shower when the curtain flew open and Star stood before me balancing a rock on the makeshift pipe. She maintained eye contact as she handed it to me but as soon as I took the hit she began to look me up and down. I trembled a bit both from the anticipation of the drug and the anticipation of her. I hit the pipe once more and inhaled deeply, leaning back against the shower wall a bit as my senses reacted and the drug pounded my brain. Star reached for me and pulled me in for a "shotgun", pressing her lips hard against mine as I blew the smoke deep into her lungs. She threw her head back while still holding me close. Both of our faces were trembling as she looked into my eyes, reached down slowly, picked up the lighter from the corner of the tub, and walked out without another word. Crack cocaine was my lover at that time. It was hers as well. The thought ran through my mind that we shared the same lover. It was erotic. And sick.

I came back out in my shorts to find Star lounging on my bed reading one of my paperbacks she'd found on the bookshelf. She seemed completely involved in what she was reading.

"You hungry or anything?" I asked.

She didn't look up. "What you got, B?"

I pulled a T-shirt from the drawer and slipped it on. "How about I order us some Chinese?"

"Very sexy. Do it."

I called in the order then went over to Star who was still

immersed in the book.

"So, you saw that I live here?"

"That's what I said."

"You're clairvoyant or something?"

She looked up into my eyes. "You want me to leave?"

"I'm glad you came."

"I get around. I know where everybody at."

"It's just that I live a good twenty miles away from Cole. I'm surprised you found me."

Star ignored me and continued to read. She slid one leg over the side of the bed and patted the mattress between her legs for me to sit down. I stared at the loose fitting boxers as I sat, with a full view of all of Star. I smiled nervously. What game was this girl playing and when exactly would I be invited to join in?

She put the book down and grabbed the pipe from the bedside table. She took a deep hit and once again pressed her lips to mine for another shotgun. I exhaled as she peered over the top of her glasses at me and smiled. Her face was trembling once again.

"You don't seem to be doing so badly out here."

"I'm not complaining. Especially at the moment."

"You like having a girl around huh?"

"If it's the right girl."

She loaded the pipe again.

"You don't have a girlfriend?"

"Not at the moment."

"I like to hang loose myself."

"You don't want any ties huh?"

"Like you say, not at the moment."

We spent the next half hour passing the pipe back and forth and giving each other shotguns. With each one our lips stayed pressed together longer and longer, becoming lingering kisses while we held each other tightly.

She looked at me intently . You know, my Mom is

white."

I smiled. "So we have something in common."

"She's Italian, I'm African American, you're neither."

The delivery man opened the door and Star became as excited as a kid on Christmas morning. She jumped up and ran for the front door, startling the young delivery guy as she swung it open wildly. His eyes went straight to her chest as she bounced with excitement. She grabbed the bag from him and ran back toward the table. I gave him his money. "Looks like she already gave you your tip," I said and closed the door.

I joined Star at the table where she was tearing open containers like a wild woman.

"Hungry?" I grinned.

She smiled seductively. "What's the matter? Can't handle eating with a strong willed woman?"

I let out a little laugh. "Sweetheart, I think I can handle anything you throw at me."

She stopped opening the food and looked over her glasses at me again. "We'll see about that."

Star walked over and grabbed the pipe again from the nightstand. She placed a huge rock on it and walked back to me, shoving me down into a recliner and straddling me. She held the flame from the lighter for me as I took the hit. I began to cough a bit and smoke was pouring out of my nose and mouth. Star pushed herself into me. "More, don't stop."

I tried not to cough as she continued to burn the rock and hold the pipe to my lips.

"Morc", she kept saying. "More."

When I had inhaled all that I possibly could she pressed her lips fiercely to mine to take in all of the exhaled smoke that she was able. She exhaled, put the pipe to her own lips and burned what was left of the rock. She kissed me lightly, dropped the pipe onto my chair, stood up and began to dance seductively in front of me with her hands up high over her head. Her entire body was shaking, as

55

was mine, and I watched her dance with wild, unblinking eyes. She glanced down at me and smiled.

Star stopped dancing abruptly, sat down at the table, and started munching on an eggroll as she went back to reading the novel. I stayed where I was, my senses completely off, my hearing as if I was in a deep tunnel, my heart pounding. Star read and ate happily as I tried to recover. Finally she spoke, without taking her eyes off of the page. "Anything I can throw at you huh boyfriend?"

I was unable to speak and she came and stood in front of me, smiling down at me again. She straddled me once again. " I don't think you can handle all that now can you?"

She reached down between my legs and began to rub me.

"Can you get your dick hard?"

She rubbed harder and began to grind into me.

"Am I getting your cock hard baby?"

She stood back up and winked at me. "No, cause you can't handle me at all. Nobody handles me."

I tried to speak but couldn't. I was pissed at my body for not cooperating with my thoughts.

"Well," she said. "That's the last of it. We smoked it all. What you wanna do B?"

I was really messed up. Star smiled at me with an almost pitying smile. She was toying with me. "What you wanna do now B?" she smiled again.

I managed to stand up and stepped to her. I put my arms around her waist and pulled her into me, leaning in for a kiss. She smiled slightly and turned her head to the side, avoiding the kiss. She whispered into my ear. "Ohhh. That's what you wanna do." Then she pulled away.

"What...what's wrong?, I stammered.

"Come on B. Let's run a mission together. We're not done yet."

I felt rejected. "Yeah, whatever."

I turned away and she grabbed me, kissing me softly on the lips.

"Don't pout boyfriend. What would your boys think?"

She let go and walked into the bathroom. Closing the door behind her.

All was silent, tense, as we drove along. I shot her a quick glance but she was looking out the passenger window.

"I don't get this Star. What's wrong?"

"Nothing's wrong. Let's just go get something."

I shook my head in confusion as she continued to stare out the window into the darkness.

"I don't have any more cash on me."

"We'll find out what's happenin' on the street."

"Shit man," I burst out. "We had enough tonight. Let's just go back to my place."

"What you thinkin' is gonna happen huh? I look like your hoe?"

"What? No! Let's just go back and get some sleep."

She smirked. "Sleep huh?"

"Jesus, I'm just trying to be your friend here."

"I know what you tryin' to be. You wanna be wit' me you better learn to respect my lifestyle."

I pulled over to a parking lot and stopped.

"I don't know what the fuck you're talking about. I'm not some goddamned street punk here. What's this? I'm not good enough?"

"What is it you want B? A relationship? Romance? Feelings? Damn!"

"For fuck's sake it was just a fuckin' kiss. Damn yourself! Can't even tell a girl you like her anymore. It's not like you weren't sticking your tongue down my throat half the night either so don't even play like I was fuckin' out of line or something."

We sat silent for a moment before Star replied.

"You like me? You know what B? You're a nice guy and you got your brand new bad ass rep and a couple of bucks left thinkin' you can still live normal. You think I don't want somebody huh? What're we gonna do B? Play house all day and hit the pipe all night?"

She turned to me and her face was wet with tears. My heart softened and I tried to calm things down a bit.

"Alright. Let's just relax a minute okay? Why don't we just take it slow for tonight and have some fun."

"My kind of fun or yours?"

"I'm hoping that sooner or later the two will mesh. I think they were already. But for now yours."

"Will you drop me off at my cousin's after? Or will I be somehow indebted to pay you back?"

"All I want is for us to get to know each other."

She smiled. "I didn't come to your place to eat Chinese. Though that shit was good."

"So we're cool?"

"Yeah, cool."

I put the car into gear and we were off and running again. I remember thinking that you could break out of the common life if you had somebody uncommon to do it with. The everyday bullshit wouldn't be so bad with somebody like Star waiting for me at home. Her energy and passion were intoxicating. She wasn't ready to hear that just yet.

The Corvette had been one of the first casualties of my job loss and subsequently I had purchased a five hundred dollar Nova from some guy who may or may not have actually owned it. I certainly wasn't about to pay insurance on it and I simply threw on some old tags that had been in my closet. I pulled the old car up to the curb in front of Cole's house and saw Star sitting on the stone wall with a young white guy about my age. The guy said something to Star and she smiled sweetly at him. I got out of the car and walked across the street to join some little girls in a game of jump rope. Star watched me intently as I took my turn jumping to the hysterical laughter of the girls. I smiled and gestured for one of the little one's to take my place. I headed back across the street toward Star and her new friend and posed my question as I got close.

"Who's this?"

"New kid on the block lookin' to cop but Doc don't trust nobody. Go get us some and the boy'll hook us up B."

The guy grinned at me. "How ya doin'?"

I kicked him so hard in the face that my leg went numb for a moment. He fell over the back of the wall with blood gushing from his nose. Star covered her eyes with her hand though she maintained a blank, emotionless expression on her face. Cole came to the door munching on a breakfast bar and called out gleefully. "Damn! Let that mutha fucka know it B!"

I kicked the guy several more times in his gut as he sobbed and tried to protect himself from the blows. I grabbed the back of his hair and yanked his head back to look in his eyes. "You come near this house again and I'll beat your ass again. You go near her again and I'll fuckin' kill you."

I shook him violently. "You hear me asshole?"

"Okay man!"

Star growled at me. "You don't own me man. Don't start thinkin' that you do."

I shot her a quick look. "Just enjoying my lifestyle baby. I know you respect that. That's what it's all about right? This fuckin' lifestyle?"

I continued up to the front door where Cole was waiting to put his arm around my shoulders. "You like a ray of sunshine on a dark winter day ain't ya boy?"

I turned back to look at Star who was still sitting on the wall with her back to us, listening to the guy behind her on the ground moaning. Cole spoke quietly into my ear.

"She don't give a shit 'bout that white bitch man. Go make up. Go give her a lil' kiss an' say I'm sorry baby. Take me back baby."

I couldn't help but smile. Cole had that way about him. He continued chewing his breakfast bar in my ear while he looked over my shoulder at Star. He took another bite, nudged me, and I called out to her.

"You comin?"

She looked at me like a bug and I pulled a long string of crack vials from my pocket, keeping them half hidden beneath my shirt.

"Are...you...coming?"

Cole sniffed. "Come on now baby doll. Lookit what he brung you. Girl's best friend. White rocks."

She got up and shuffled toward us. I reached out my hand and she took it.

"Look what I did," Cole smiled. "She happy again."

We went back inside where Junior had been standing and watching everything from the front window.

"Yo B man," he chided. "I ain't never touched her man. Never even looked at the girl. Don't talk to her...don't think about her."

Cole bent over in exaggerated laughter. Junior shook his head. "Boy's crazy man."

"Hear dat," Cole agreed. "Jus' like her."

Moments later we were back in the attic and everyone took their regular seats. Star stayed away from me, clearly on purpose, and went to sit beside Cole on the bed.

Cole lightly elbowed her. "Don't you wanna sit wit' your man?"

"Who says he's my man?"

"I jus' don't want him fuckin' me up for sittin' wit' ya.

What you fightin' 'bout anyway?"

Star shrugged. "We was cool till he show up like Bruce Lee kickin' people an' shit."

Cole turned to me. "You wanna express yourself?"

"Looked to me like he jus' did," Junior said.

Cole changed the subject. "You know there ain't nothin' to eat in this house but them damn crunch bars?"

"You never heard there's children starving in Africa?" I smirked.

"There's African's starving in America. Shut the fuck up. I'm trying to save your marriage here."

We all laughed and I held my hand up. "Doc?"

"What?"

"Can we smoke now?"

"Hell, yeah." Star agreed.

She got up and came to sit beside me. I felt a rush go through me and hoped that it wasn't too obvious to everyone else. Cole smiled a little and pulled out his pipe. He winked at me as he loaded it.

Are you a nigger? Are you that only care about yourself drain on society that I keep hearing about? Are you that person that I don't want to see in my neighborhood or my church or sitting next to my child in the classroom? Are you the one who brings down my property values and costs me a promotion because of affirmative action? Are you that child I will not adopt because of what people might say? Or the friend I'll never have because people might point? Or the woman I'll never love because people might stare? Are you that nigger?"

Every now and then we felt the need to get outside as a group and soak up some sun. Most of our days were spent behind locked doors or running our little missions in the dark, but today was different. We were gathered in Cole's backyard where the boom- box was blasting out "Down with OPP". Star was dancing and chewing on an apple. She'd yell out, "Yeah you know me!" whenever the line came on. Cole, Junior, Con, Joe and I were playing badminton with rackets and a birdie but no net. Cole sat in his lawn chair behind dark glasses with a cigarette dangling from his lips. He held the racket in one hand and a barbecue fork in the other as he rolled hot dogs on the small charcoal grill. Every time the birdie came close enough he'd swat it forcefully like he was trying to kill it.

Two young guys came walking into the yard approached Cole. He pushed one of them out of his way so he wouldn't miss the birdie. They handed him some cash and he produced a few vials from his pocket. Star saw me watching her dance and began to dance a bit more sexy. I stopped dead and stared at her. I felt a sudden surge of determination and headed for her quickly. Our eyes locked and she opened her arms out wide, calling to me as I approached."

"What?"

I continued toward her.

"What you got, huh?" She grinned. "Bring it!"

As I closed in her expression grew serious. ""That's the look I wanna see on a man's face when he look at me."

I grabbed her and kissed her passionately. She caressed my neck and we fell to the ground giggling like kids. There comes a time in all of our lives when we have to choose between what's right and what's wrong. Not for the whole world, just for ourselves. Sometimes the world will disagree with our decision. But fuck the world. I took her by the hand and ran with her back into the house. Cole smiled and bent over to turn the hot dogs as the birdie hit him in the head.

Chapter Three: The Spiral

Cole and I walked along one of the crumbling sidewalks which could be found throughout this part of town. Junior, Con and Joe trailed behind, playing around with fake karate kicks and slap fighting. All of us wore dark shades to shield us from the very bright sun which at this point was not at all our friend. Cole's stood out as always. He had found some Jimi Hendrix looking glasses which were almost purplish in color and had very big, round lenses. Between those and his baby blue sport coat he was a genuine attraction to see. People moved instinctively out of his way and one young woman pulled her child quickly aside as if he might be in harm's way. A middle aged black man passed us and Cole raised his fist in a black power salute. The man ignored him.

"Let's go downtown," Joe said. "Ain't nobody out here man."

Cole spit. "Quit whinin' bitch."

Junior jogged up to us. "How 'bout it Doc? We can mission with B's car."

Con agreed. "Sounds good to me y'all."

"No more money in the bank huh?" Cole asked me.

"Not a dime. So what do we got? Forty bucks?"

"Long way down for forty," he agreed.

Joe continued to whine. "Next time you guys got, you should share."

Cole turned to Con. "I'll give you the forty if you kill his ass."

Con smiled. "He jus' bein' hisself."

"So we on, or what?" Junior asked.

Cole turned to me. "Your car B."

"I got half a tank. Lotta gas for only forty but fuck it

let's go."

"Morer for the money downtown anyway." Junior added.

We turned and began to walk back toward my car which we'd left on the corner two blocks back. Cole turned to me. "Been meanin' to ask man, what happened to the nice car?"

"Repo man."

"Damn."

"Yeah."

"That shit had a stereo with some kick man."

"Yeah."

"And those leather seats was nice man."

"Yeah."

"Shit."

"Yeah."

A car suddenly came up quickly from behind us and

screeched to a stop. Demond and three other guys jumped out wielding utility razor blades and baseball bats. Demond rushed me, slicing wildly from side to side and I raised my arms boxer style to protect my face. He began to slice up my arms and the stinging pain shot through me. Cole, Junior and Con were fighting furiously with the other three. Joe took off running. Con got a bat away from one of the other men and began to beat him viciously with it. Cole got behind another guy, grabbing the arm he held the knife with and reaching behind him for his own gun. He grabbed it and called out to me.

"B, right here man!"

I turned to see Cole toss the gun but I was unable to catch it as I fought to defend myself against Demond. The gun fell into some tall weeds beside the road. Junior finished helping Con pound two of the attackers into a bloody mess before running over to pull Demond off of me where we were wrestling on the ground for control of the blade. Junior slammed Demond's head into the roof of his car, threw him to the ground, and began kicking him wildly in the midsection. Cole was slicing up the third guy's face and yelling, "How you like that huh? How you like that bitch!"

Cole slapped him hard, sending blood spraying from his face, then let him and one of the other attackers run for their car and speed away. They left Demond and another man who were lying motionless on the ground.

"They dead?" Junior asked.

Cole bent down to check. "Naw, jus' sorry."

He picked up his gun from the grass and walked back to me to check my wounds. "Nuthin' deep B. Hurt like shit later though."

It was then we noticed Con holding his blood soaked hands together.

"Oh shit man," I yelled, "Are you alright?"

"Muthafucka cut my thumb near off man. Fuck!"

He bent over with the pain, clutching his injured hand to his belly.

I turned to Cole. "He's gotta get to a hospital."

"I'll run down for your ride," he answered.

I fumbled for my keys and handed them to Cole who took off running down the block. Junior and I supported Con as best we could. After a minute Cole came flying up with the car and we carefully helped Con into the front seat. Cole got out and walked over to Demond who was still out for the count. He knelt down and pressed his palms down over his cousin's nose until it broke and blood began to flow. Cole placed his hands on either side of Demond's face, leaning down and kissing him on the forehead. When he stood back up Demond's blood was all over him.

"Stay outta my hood cuz. I fuckin' told you already."

Junior pulled him away. "Let's go man! Cops will be comin'."

They stumbled back to the car and Junior hopped in back with me. Cole wiped the blood from his face with his sleeve, took one last look back at Demond, then jumped back in the driver seat and sped us away. At that moment I realized this was a war. Life on the street was like life on a battlefield. I was a rookie soldier and Cole was a seasoned general. Breaking his cousin's nose was more for me to see than an act of malice toward Demond. Cole's way of letting us all know who he truly considered to be family.

Junior, Cole and I sat drinking beer and nursing our wounds in the attic. It had grown dark outside and the neighborhood was beginning to come to life. There was dried blood all over our clothes and skin. My arms were wrapped up in some old white bath towels Cole had grabbed for me. The blood had stained through. Star came bounding up the steps and covered her mouth with her hand when she saw us.

"Oh my God. Are you guys alright?"

"Yeah," Cole answered. "But Con hurt pretty bad."

She turned to me. "B? You okay baby?"

"Enjoying my lifestyle," I mumbled.

Star lowered her eyes, obviously hurt, and she turned to leave. I was immediately sorry and took her arm softly.

"Star wait. I'm sorry. Please sit down."

She took a seat on an old milk crate and stayed strangely quiet. We sat in silence for about ten minutes before Joe came up. Anger flashed in Cole's eyes as he jumped to his feet.

"Where'd you go to blood?"

Joe stammered. "I...I'm sorry man. Doc, I came back. I just freaked an' shit."

"You left us wit' heat on bitch. Jus' like a lil' fuckin' bitch!"

Joe pulled a large bag of cocaine from his pocket. "I went downtown man. I got two ounces fronted from Hector."

I looked up horrified. "Oh my God. Not our Hector."

Junior stood up. "Are you crazy man? Are you out your fuckin' mind? How you gonna pay?"

Joe waved us off. "No, no, don't sweat it. My Mom's got these savings bonds she bought for me when I was a kid. She's ginin' 'em to me to cash in."

Cole was clearly rattled. "How much?"

"Two ounces," Joe answered.

"No you fucked up nigger! How much are the bonds worth?"

Joe stuttered. "Fi...five, five hundred."

I closed my eyes. "That's not enough."

Joe smiled a reassuring smile. "No, it's cool though B. We made a deal. Five in two days and the rest by the end of the month."

"Today's the twenty-sixth you fuckin' moron! We're all fuckin' dead!"

Cole became frantic. "Why'd you go to our boy? Who told you to go to our boy?"

"He's the only guy I know. He's my boy too."

"Like talkin' to a bitch," Cole answered. "He only your boy cause we drag your sorry fuckin' ass around wit' us."

Joe looked desperate. "Come on Doc, look at all of this."

I tried to steer things into business mode. "Alright, okay. We can work with this. We'll put a little aside for ourselves and sell the rest at a profit. That should give us plenty to pay him back."

Cole shook his head. "You had to go to the fuckin' Dominican man? You better be for real wit' these bonds."

Joe turned to Star. "I don't give up my shit to no bitch that don't suck my dick."

Before Star could respond, pure rage overtook me and I jumped to my feet. "I will fuckin' kill you right here boy!"

Joe backed away quickly. "Okay, cool B. She in."

"You're too fuckin' dumb to be stupdi," Cole shot at

him. "Give me that shit. It ain't yours muthafucka."

I sat back down and my eyes locked with Star's. She mouthed the words, "I love you," the first time she'd ever let me know. I gestured for her to come over and she sat down on my lap very gingerly. I whispered in her ear that I loved her too and kissed her lips softly. Joe moved over to the table, keeping his eye on me and more importantly on Cole who was much more likely to kill him. Cole poured a gram of the coke into a small glass jar and added a small bit of baking soda and water. He lit a flame underneath and swirled the mixture slowly until we heard a tapping from inside the cloudy little jar. He drained the excess fluid into a paper towel, revealing a nice sized cooked rock. He dumped it out onto a mirror and cut it into tiny little pieces. Joe loaded a piece into a pipe and handed it to me.

"Peace man. We alright?"

"Ladies first," I answered with a nod.

Joe went to hand the pipe to Star. She looked at Cole for

approval. He nodded.

Star hit the pipe and her face changed instantly. This was potent stuff. Joe stared at her, licked his lips, and shifted position where he sat on the floor to try and hide his arousal. I didn't notice but Cole did.

"You better get your mind on somethin' else boy," he threatened.

I caught on. "You testing me?"

"No man. Sorry. Cool okay?"

I glared at him until he lowered his eyes like a dog. Cole looked toward me.

"'Nough B."

"What was that?" I asked

"Chill the fuck out," he spat back.

"Are you on a bad trip maybe? Thinkin' you're my Mama?"

Cole looked down into the mirror. He ran his fingers

through his hair. ""I'm too good lookin' to be your Mama. Ugly ass crackhead. Fuck you."

I looked at him hard for a moment and he raised his eyes to meet my stare. A silent tension filled the room for a moment before we both burst into laughter. Junior laughed along nervously.

"Damn! ?I was gettin' ready to head for the door yo."

Star was clearly bugged out and paranoid. She squeezed into the chair beside me and held onto my arm. Her eyes darted about quickly. I kissed her forehead and whispered into her ear. "You're okay. It's me. I won't let anything happen."

Star forced a weak smile but couldn't speak.

"Shit stonger'n around here," Cole added

"We need to cut it a bit more. Or else we'll all lose our shit."

Cole nodded. "Yeah."

Joe loaded the pipe again and went to hand it to me.

"A little blow instead man," I asked.

He set the pipe aside and scooped a little of the sifted powder into a matchbook cover and handed it to me with a short straw. I snorted half of it and handed the rest to Cole who finished it. I had the same reaction as Star. The purity of the drug overpowered me.

Joe decided that it was a good time to exert himself. "What now B? You don't look so fuckin' tough now bitch. Wanna step outside wit' it?"

Cole pulled a gun from behind his back and pointed it right at Joe's head. "I'll go."

Joe fell backward to the floor and tried to cover up with his arms. His eyes went from the gun barrel to Cole's face and back again.

"Damn man! I was jus' playin'."

Cole kept the gun on him another long moment. "You better fukin' be."

"Shit man. You didn't point no gun at B."

"Cole looked at him. "Cause I like B."

Junior and I started laughing. Cole looked at how bugged out I was and laughed half with me and half at me.

"You back with me bro?"

I nodded yes, still unable to speak.

"You never really gone are you?" He turned to Joe. "Boy's dangerous all the time."

Joe glanced quickly at me then back down to the mirror on the table. Cole turned on the boom box and TLC's "What about your friends" came on.

Cole smiled. "You see these crazy bitches wearin' rubbers all over their clothes an' eyes an' shit?"

"It's inviting," I said.

"Invitin? To a rubbermaid salesman maybe."

We all began to crack up laughing to the point of tears and shortness of breath. We couldn't seem to stop no matter what we tried. Cole was near tears.

"Shit ain't that funny!" he yelled.

He only made us laugh all the more, with Junior rolling over to the floor hysterical.

"Good shit!" Star yelled.

"You're welcome," Joe fumed.

The sun was beginning to shine through my blinds by the time I reached home but otherwise it was pretty dim. I glanced into the mirror and looked absolutely awful. I was still wearing the same blood soaked clothes and my face was gray and sickly looking. I collapsed on my bed a second before someone knocked on my door.

"Shit."

The knocking continued and I rolled myself out of the bed, grabbed the gun Cole had given me from my dresser, and proceeded to open the door. Once again it was the expressionless face of Star.

"You following me?"

"Can't help myself."

"You know, you could just tell me you want to come with me when I'm leaving Cole's."

"Yeah."

"Come in."

She looked down at the gun in my hand then studied my worried face for a long moment.

"We smoked it all didn't we?"

"Except for an eight-ball I saved for you and me."

"What now? How do you pay Hector?"

I could only shrug.

Star paced around slowly, looking at some of the books on my shelf.

"Offer still open to crash here?"

86

"Always, or until someone kills me, whichever comes first. You really should tell me when you want to come over so you can ride with me. Consider it your place too okay?"

"Okay."

I took her hand and led her toward the bed.

"I'm exhausted."

"Crazy too. Go take your grungy ass into the shower."

I smiled, kissed her hand softly, and headed into the bathroom to comply.

A few minutes later I was getting out of the shower and wrapping a towel around my waist. I tilted my head back to look into my nostrils which were very red and swollen. Star entered, pushed me aside and opened the medicine cabinet. She grabbed some peroxide and cotton balls.

"Sit", she ordered.

I took a seat on the toilet as Star poured some peroxide on a cotton ball and began to gently dab at the cuts on my arms.

"Man! Shit!"

She jumped back with a wide smile.

"Oh boy, you are a badass ain't ya?"

"Fuck you. That shit hurts."

"Stop being a pussy. It's gonna get infected. Sit there and take it like a man."

She dabbed some more and grinned as I grimaced.

When Star had finished playing nurse we went back into the main room and I grabbed the bag of coke I had saved for us. I poured a little baking soda into the bag as well, shook it up a bit, then used a strainer from the kitchen to refine it. A pile of nice powder began to form on the table. The process turned an eight-ball, three and one half grams, into nearly four and a half. The coke was pure enough to cut that much and still be outstanding. I put a little on my finger and rubbed it on Star's lips. I leaned over and kissed her and she smiled. I cut some lines with a razor blade and we each snorted two lines up each nostril.

The stuff hit us hard and fast once again and I became very paranoid. I got up to peek through the blinds and Star put her finger over her lips to say "Shhh." She went to check the blinds at the other end of the room. We were very freaked out but sat back down to do some more. I snorted another line and my nose began to bleed down onto my chest. A tiny bit of blood dripped into the pile of coke but that didn't stop Star from snorting it. We continued like that for a long while, nervous and shaking but never thinking to stop. Never once thinking to stop.

Hours later I awoke on the hard floor with Star asleep beside me. I got up and walked to the bathroom, just then noticing I was still wearing the towel around my waist. I knelt in front of the toilet motionless, then threw up a white chemical looking fluid into the bowl. I began to cough and gag, holding my stomach which I now realized hurt quite a bit. I felt another rush come on and threw up a bit of blood. Star came in and knelt down beside me, rubbing my back. She leaned me back to rest on her chest, stroking my hair and humming.

"Just too much without eating anything baby."

She continued to hum and hold me for a while.

"You're okay baby....you're okay."

Addicts live a life of near constant fear and deep emptiness. For one addict to consider another a brother, and a woman almost a part of himself, only happened once that I know of. For the most part they cannot be consoled. They remain independent and trust no one. No one is allowed inside. They are diseased.

Does this disease make them the trash the world despises?

Cole was sitting out on the stone wall in front of his

house when Star and I pulled up and got out of the car. He lit a cigarette and nodded.

"What up?"

"The sky," Star answered. She walked on into the house, banging the screen door behind her as always. I sat down beside Cole.

"You fuck her yet?" he asked.

I just smiled.

He shook his head. "You ain't done nothing. Not even smart enough to lie."

"Nope."

"We should go into the city for some professional pussy."

"Maybe so," I nodded.

"We're all gonna die tomorrow anyway if Joe don't produce those fuckin' bonds." "You see him yet?"

Cole shook his head no.

"You understand that he's gonna hold us responsible?"

Cole didn't respond.

"We got no money to get anything in the city anyway," I added.

"Mmm, Hmm, follow me, I know a dude."

We walked to a building about halfway down the block and entered when the buzzer sounded. "Right back," Cole said and headed up the steps while I sat down on the stoop and lit a smoke. A homeless man approached and studied me for a moment.

"I know you."

"That right?"

"Demond offerin' cash to any nigga who smoke your ass."

I took a drag on my smoke and smiled at him. Demond ain't got no cash and you're too smart to try me."

"Hear dat."

He walked on and I grinned to myself. Someday I'd have to write a book I thought.

After a few minutes a fairly attractive white girl came out of the building, sweating heavily. Her eyes were wild and I could tell she was racing. She nodded to me.

"Hey."

"You want a blowjob for ten bucks?"

I looked her up and down, glanced up quickly toward the building windows, then grabbed her by the hand and took her back into the alley. She knelt down in front of me and began to open my belt.

When I came back out of the alley Cole was sitting on the front stoop. The girl came running out a few seconds later clutching the money in her hand. She ran to the front door, pushed a button, and waited for the buzzer. Cole looked her over.

"Shit's that desperate huh? Hey, how 'bout me girl?"

The door buzzed and she ignored him, quickly running

up the steps.

"You're too fuckin' ugly," I said.

"My Daddy's fault."

We walked back toward Cole's house. Cole smiled up into the sky. "Couldn't do it could you?"

"No."

"Mmmm, Hmmm."

"Too much thinking. I felt sorry for her. Plus I kinda got something started with Star."

"Yeah."

"Ever happen to you?"

"Hell no."

I laughed and we walked in silence a moment.

"Maybe," he said.

Minutes later we were back in the attic smoking the pipe. "Your girl can't be patient a damn hour," Cole mumbled. "Off runnin' the streets when we have the shit right here."

I was too messed up to answer. I looked up at him and nodded.

"I know you hear me."

Cole took another hit as I stood up and walked to the corner. I sat down on the floor between a chair and the wall, closing myself off. Cole pointed at me.

"Don't start gettin' fuckin' paranoid now." He closed his eyes. "Though I do know what you mean."

The light in the room suddenly went very dim. Cole was speaking to me but I couldn't hear him, only distant mumbling. I reached out for the wall, the chair, anything. I felt like I was falling. My heart was pounding and I grabbed my chest. Cole jumped up and moved toward me. "Oh fuck, oh fuck, oh…" Then silence.

I thought I was going to die. I remember thinking If I died in Cole's house he'd be in trouble with the police. I remember thinking I didn't want Star to see my dead body. I remember asking God to help me and thinking it

95

wouldn't do any good. God wasn't in any damn crack house waiting to take requests.

I opened my eyes to a stream of cold water hitting me in the face. Cole and Junior were standing over me and Cole was holding a garden hose. I was lying in the backyard completely soaked. Cole looked worried.

"You alright man?"

"What happened?"

"You went down for the count bro. I ran next door for Junior an' we carried your ass out here."

Junior knelt down beside me. "You okay B?"

"Everything's spinning. I think I'm alright."

"I tested that shit man. There's heavy speed in that shit."

Cole growled. "Wait'll I catch the mutha fucka's again. I'll fuckin' kill 'em.Scare a nigga half to death."

I rested on the sofa in the living room with Star beside me, worriedly patting my head with a damp cloth. Cole sat resting his head on the back of his easy chair, staring at the ceiling. I turned to him.

"How's Con doing?"

"They were able to save his thumb. Gotta stay in there a few more days."

"Good."

Star lowered her head to my chest. I put my arms around her and she looked up into my eyes. All was quiet.

"You see Joe yet," I asked.

"No," Cole answered.

"Time's up tomorrow."

"Yeah."

As the evening came on we just sat like that in silence. Junior was out front watching the strangely silent street and the three of us right where we were staring at the ceiling. Nobody got high that night. Nobody smoked or drank or moved. We hardly slept at all. We'd had some asshole almost poison us with a bad batch. Demond was looking to pay someone to shoot us. And there was a Dominican heavyweight that would be looking to dump us in the river by the end of the next day. Con was in the hospital and Joe was nowhere to be found. That left me, Cole, Junior, and a very frightened female. Who am I fooling, we were all frightened. Somewhere in the middle of the night Cole muttered something about us having to pack heat from now on. I didn't answer him. I think he was talking to himself.

I fell asleep early in the morning, waking to the feel of warm sunshine on my face. I was alone on the sofa and the room was empty. I heard some commotion outside and sat up to look out the window. There were police cars a few doors down at Joe's house and a large group including Cole, Junior and Star had formed on the lawns of the other houses to learn what was happening. I walked out into the cool morning air to join them and it was then that I saw Joe's mother and sister across the street. Both were in tears and clutching one another close. I walked over to stand beside the others.

"What's going on?"

"Joe's dead," Junior answered flatly.

I felt instantly sick to my stomach. "Dead?"

"His sister say he hung hisself in the closet."

We stood there quiet for a few minutes, all of us trying to absorb this information and what it might mean. Cole turned to me and spoke softly.

"We gotta be ready."

"Cops is sayin' suicide," Junior told me. "But Joe's sister is sayin' there wasn't no chair or nuthin'. How'd he pull that shit off?"

Cole frowned. "Hector."

"Don't sound good man," Junior agreed.

"He'll come for us next."

"We'll go to him first," I interjected.

The others turned to look at me in disbelief.

"You're fuckin' crazy," Star said.

"No. We go to him first. We don't know anything about this shit. We haven't seen Joe since he ran away from the fight the other day. We go down to cop like nothing's up."

Junior shook his head. "I dunno B."

Cole rubbed his chin. "How can the fuckin' Five-O say suicide man?"

"His sister says there was a note," Junior answered. "Talkin' about how he can't live like this no more an' shit like that."

I thought for a moment. "Maybe he did kill himself. Even if he didn't, if Hecot did this he was right across the street for fuck's sake. Why'd he let us go? Maybe he doesn't hold us responsible?"

Cole shook his head again. "No fuckin' way man. We're

in this shit deep. He jus' wants his money is all. And you know he wants a whole lotta interest."

"Maybe the boy killed hisself," Star repeated.

"Then let's find out," I answered. "I'd rather get it over with than have to look over my shoulder twenty-four-seven."

"Alright," Cole said. "But if we goin', we goin' down packin'."

"We go down with nothing," I said. No reason to, right? We don't know a damn thing about any of this. We have no reason at all to fear our friend Hector. We're just there to cop like any other day, that's it. We all think Joe killed himself like the note says." I looked across the street at Joe's sobbing mother. "We need to get some money fast."

Within an hour Cole and I were carrying my television and some other items out of my place to the car. We pawned them quickly at a local shop and pocketed a few hundred bucks. We went back to Cole's attic to make our plans and get our stories together. When we came back downstairs Star was sitting on the sofa looking terrified.

"We're going."

She nodded.

Cole walked to her and kissed her forehead. "If I don't come back you go to the hospital and tell Con to get outta town. You go wit' him."

She lowered her head into her hands and I went to kneel down in front of her.

"Look at me."

She didn't move,

"Please Star, look at me."

She opened her hands and looked at me through teary eyes."

"We'll be back in a couple of hours okay?"

She nodded halfheartedly."

"Okay?"

"Okay."

"If you're a good girl while we're away I'll bring you back a shiny new crack pipe."

Star laughed a little through her tears. We embraced and looked into each other's eyes. I kissed her softly then walked out the door followed by Cole and Junior.

Star would later say that at that moment I became everything she wanted me to be. That sometimes what you think of as freedom is really imprisonment. The thought occurred to her that had she just said the word we'd both be out. She knew at the same time it wasn't true. It was too late now. We were cell mates, counting away the days until someone finally threw the switch on us.

An hour later we pulled up across from Hector's run down apartment building in the inner city. We sat for a few minutes watching two heavily armed guards pace in front of the building's entrance. Though none of us said it, I knew we were all considering the fact that these might be the last few moments of our lives. A grand was nothing to Hector, except that it was a helluva example to make to others who might think about stealing from him. My hands shook as I lit a cigarette and took a deep drag.

"Shit."

"Mmm, Hmm." Cole took the smoke from me, took a drag, and flicked it out the window. "Let's go."

We climbed out and made our way across the street toward the guards. Cole spoke quietly. "Much love brothers."

"Right on," Junior replied, and then we were there.

Cole nodded to the guards. "What up?"

We had never been patted down on the street before but somehow the rules had changed. They checked us thoroughly before motioning for us to go on up. Cole led the way with his usual swaggering style followed by Junior and then me. We climbed the several flights of steps carefully avoiding the vomit and other grotesque substances that covered them. The walls were covered with gang graffiti and a young woman about twenty was sprawled out on one of the landings looking like she was convulsing. She was nude from the waist up. When we reached the third floor landing Cole knocked on the door. A young Hispanic man answered and patted us down once more. We had only been patted down one time in the past, and certainly never twice in one visit. He stepped aside for us to enter.

It was a dark and dingy apartment. A statue of the virgin Mary sat on a table just inside the foyer with candles burning around it. There was nothing else in the place save for an old sofa and a metal folding table. Hector sat in a swivel office chair behind it, staring out the window. Cole spoke first. "What's up Hector?"

He kept his back to us. "You come to paya me?"

"What?" Cole asked evenly.

Hector turned around and faced us.

105

"To paya. Come to paya, no?"

"Huh?"

Hector became agitated. "Come on!"

Cole looked straight at him. "I don't get it. What's up?"

"De money for Joe, yes?"

Cole turned to Junior and I. We shrugged.

"My money for Joe!" Hector yelled.

"What fuckin' money?" Cole yelled back.

"Two fuckin' ounce!"

"What! Speaking fuckin' English."

I stepped forward, digging in my pocket. "Hector we don't understand." I pulled out some cash. "We just came for an eight-ball. Is something wrong?"

Hector looked at his man who shrugged as if he didn't know what the hell was going on. Hector's eyes were calculating. He was debating with himself.

"You no see Joe?"

"I know you haven't heard Hector, but Joe killed himself. We hadn't seen him for a little while, I guess he was pretty depressed."

He searched my eyes for a moment for the truth, looked at the money in my hand, glanced at Cole and Junior, then pulled out a bag of coke. He emptied some onto a scale. He pulled out a knife, looked at Cole, then pushed some into a smaller bag which he held out for me. I gave him the cash but didn't move away.

"Are we okay Hector?"

He folded his arms and stared hard at me a moment before waving his arm flamboyantly. "Okay, go."

We exited the building and walked to the car at a leisurely pace. Cole and Junior climbed in while I glanced up toward Hector's window. Hector stood there watching us. I nodded, he smiled. I got into the car and was the first to speak.

"I think we're okay."

"Naw," Junior replied. "He ain't goin' for it. He jus'

bidin' his time."

"Drive," Cole said.

I started the car and drove down to the corner. Cole wiped his forehead.

"Turn the corner and stop."

I did as he asked and pulled over to the curb. Cole got out, stood there a moment, then bent over and vomited all over the sidewalk. He wiped his face and got back in the car.

"Home."

It was over fast I know. That's the way it is on the street. You never know where you stand. You can't ever let your guard down. Never assume you're safe.

Star sat on the sofa, glasses down low on her nose,

reading a mystery novel. Anyone who saw her would think she looked like a librarian. Someone knocked on Cole's front door and she got up to peek out the window. She opened the door to a large black man about thirty-five years old. He was fairly well dressed.

"You from the County?"

"No I ain't from no County bitch. My nigga's say i can cop up in here."

"You're too big a nigger not to be Five-O."

"Who here?"

"Nobody. Don't know what the fuck you talkin' about."

He pushed her aside the house and began to search around with Star right on his tail.

"You're no cop. What the fuck you think you're doin?"

The big man snarled. "I walk all the way up here for nuthin? Bad business."

He looked Star up and down, grabbed her by her shirt

and pulled her into him. He licked up the side of her face. "Maybe not for nuthin'."

Star tried desperately to break free. The man backhanded her across the face, sending her glasses flying. Her knees buckled and she started to fall backwards. He pulled her back to him, placed his face to hers and growled. "You gonna suck my dick bitch so stop fightin' 'fore you get dead."

Star sobbed and began to fight once more to free herself. He slapped her face a few more times viciously then shoved her down onto her knees. Blood ran from her cheek and mouth as he opened his pants and grabbed the back of her head.

"Suck it hoe."

The street was quiet as Cole, Junior and I climbed back

out of the car in front of Cole's house. We approached the house and noticed it was dark, which it never was. We grew concerned and searched around the yard a bit for something to use as a weapon. Cole grabbed an empty wine bottle from the grass and held it like a club. We entered the front door slowly and could hear Star sobbing in the darkness. Junior reached under a lamp shade and flicked on the light. She was lying in the corner in a fetal position, with a swollen eye and blood smeared face. Junior nearly turned white. "Oh man, oh man."

I walked to her slowly and knelt down beside her, gently wrapping my arms around her. She clutched me tightly and cried harder which seemed to cause her more pain. Tears flowed from my own eyes as I tried to comfort her. "Shh, I'm here. You're safe now."

Cole's face looked like a volcano about to erupt. He muttered to himself as he watched us in complete horror. He was trembling with rage, clenching and unclenching his fists. He grabbed the back of his neck as if trying to stop his own shaking.

"Who did this? Who did this?"

He rushed suddenly to the screen door, kicked it open and ran outside into the middle of the street, screaming wildly.

"Who did this! Who the fuckin' nigger who did this!You fuckin' bitch! Come try me bitch! Come try me muth fucka!"

Junior rushed from the house and tried to grab Cole who started swinging wildly as he approached. Junior backed away. Cole screamed like a madman into the sky.

"WHO DID THIS?"

He dropped his arms to his sides, lowered his head, and sobbed. Junior approached again as Cole dropped to his knees exhausted. "Who did this? She's like my Sister man."

Junior knelt down beside him and rested his head against Cole's. Cole sobbed harder.

"I know," Junior said through his own tears.

"Like my lil' Sister."

"I know."

"Gonna kill the nigger."

"I know."

Half an hour later we were at the hospital. Cole leaned against a wall in the hallway while Junior and I paced in a nearby waiting room. Rapists, hate groups, abusers, whoever. How can you look in the eyes of another human being and want to inflict that kind of suffering? There is a place where black and white cease to exist. There is only right and wrong. Were we addicted? Yes. Did this beautiful and spirited young woman do anything to deserve such punishment? Jesus no.

An older, distinguished looking black doctor approached Cole.

"My name's Doctor Lee Durham. You know who did this brother?"

Cole looked down at his feet. "Naw."

"Come on! This girl's been hurt. You must…"

Cole met his gaze. "You'll hear about it on the news when I find out…brother."

I walked over and joined them.

"Is she alright Doctor? Did he rape her?"

"She was hurt pretty bad. You know who did this?"

"No."

"Of course not."

Cole glared at him. "Let's go B."

"Can I stay with her tonight?" I asked.

"Sorry son, family only."

"She doesn't have any family. We're her family."

The Doctor studied our faces and sighed. "You can sleep in the chair in her room."

Cole sat alone in the attic drinking and staring off into nowhere, tears streaming down his face. Junior sat out on the wall in front of the house watching the quiet street. Con laid in his hospital bed staring at the ceiling and trying to absorb the devastating news Junior had brought him earlier. I sat beside Star gently stroking her arm as she slept. Doctor Durham entered and took a seat in the corner. He overturned a small no smoking sign on the table and lit his pipe. He studied me for a moment.

"We haven't been properly introduced. I'm Doctor Lee Durham, Emergency Medical Physician here at the hospital."

I remained silent, looking only at Star's battered face.

"And you are?" He asked.

"My name's Benny."

"Short for Benjamin?"

"Just Benny."

115

We sat quietly for a few moments. The Doctor motioned toward Star.

"She's very beautiful."

"Yes."

"I presume you two are courting?"

I had to smile. "Yeah. Courting."

"An old fashioned word I guess. Can words be old fashioned? It'd be quite sad to lose some of them don't you think?"

"I guess so."

"Young folks today, they're involved, seeing each other, going out. Courting is just a better word."

I smiled again. "Yes Sir."

He returned my smile and went back to puffling on his pipe as he watched us.

"You know, I'm a bit older than people might suppose."

I glanced at him. "I suppose you're pretty old."

The Doctor laughed a little, causing him to cough.

"I retired a few years back. Followed the normal course you might say. The expected course. Out early enough to play golf and travel and explore new ideas, new ways of life. There were so many possibilities you understand?"

"I guess."

"Well, I'm from these streets Benny. I'm part of them and they're a part of me. We have this wonderful love-hate relationship in that I love the history we've shared together and the memories I carry with me and yet I hate what these streets are doing to young people like you and Miss Star. They've betrayed me I'd have to say. Broken my heart more times than any woman would ever have the chance.

"So why'd you come back?"

"Because I want to beat the streets down like the bastard dogs they've become. Beat them back until they're in a place where kids can play on them and couples can

117

stroll on them and old folks reminisce on them. This was a great city once. A place you could dream and this is no fairy tale, you listen to me. But first heroin, then all the pills and now these little rocks that men trade their very salvation for. Trade their love and compassion and future and all those possibilities for. God damn son. Explain that to me."

"I can't Sir."

"Can't or won't?"

I turned to look him in the eye. "Look, I appreciate everything you're doing but..."

"You don't appreciate anything young man. You're so sad and your friend Mister Coleman is so angry. Oh Lord you have no idea how much you have and how much you've thrown away. Your sadness is the direct result of your own actions Benny. And Mister Coleman, boiling over with anger disguised as cleverness when we can clearly see the cunning way in which he thinks and the bitterness with which he lives. He needs help. You all do."

"You're the one who sounds angry Doctor."

"Just sit quiet a moment and allow me to finish. Perhaps you'll hear something you can use."

He pulled on his pipe a few more times before continuing. "I've buried three beautiful women. My mother, my wife, and my daughter. My daughter wasn't much older than you. Filled her body with garbage she injected with filthy needles. She wasted away to nothing then bit her own tongue off. I buried a skeleton. Wasn't even her lying in that box it was a stranger that stole my child. I hated her so much for that."

"You couldn't save your daughter so you came back to save everybody else."

"Couldn't save my daughter, couldn't save my father who sacrificed the very small amount of freedom he actually had and chained himself to a bottle. Couldn't save the many fine people who fell prey to the promise of pain relief offered by every corner liquor store in every poor neighborhood in this city. Couldn't save the kids lying in some mucky gutter like rabid dogs. But I'm back to try again. What I can't understand son, is why are you here?"

"My friends are here."

"Perhaps. You know, there are a handful of us who have dedicated our lives to getting young black children out of the ghettos and projects and war zones and elevating them to new challenges, possibilities and healthy ways of life. Trying to help them prosper and find real happiness. Now this rock cocaine becomes so popular I think we'll be making a second trip back so all the white kids don't get left behind. That's not fair son. Not to us, not to yourself."

"So I'm supposed to just take off and leave my friends?"

"You're supposed to prove that you care. Sometimes that means setting the hard example. I'll say this though, one addict cannot save another. You will only destroy one another."

He stood and uprighted the no smoking sign. Then

walked slowly to the doorway.

"However, should you decide to stay, you will find that I am here as well. As addicted to a romantic dream as you are to those chemicals. I will not leave until the last of you young people has left. Then I shall retire to days of golf and travel and leisure."

He turned and left without another word.

I sat on Cole's sofa with Star's head resting on my lap. She was wearing a t-shirt and shorts and her face was still badly   bruised.
I was dressed in a double breasted suit and silk tie, all that remained of my former career. Across the street and down a few doors people were arriving at Joe's house in dark clothing. It was his funeral day. Junior was in the backyard cutting Cole's hair with a pair of barber's clippers attached

to an extension cord from the kitchen. They were both wearing white shirts and dress pants. Con, also well dressed, sat on the decrepit back deck watching them from behind his dark shades. His hand was still bandaged and would be for some time. He got bored and came into the living room to sit with us.

African American's take their funerals very seriously. They're more somber and respectful. Seems that way to me anyhow. They vent their grief and allow the world to see it. Let's face it, in a place like this they got a lot more practice. Cole gave orders that morning that there were to be no drugs in the neighborhood that day.

Star stared at the ceiling and tried to sound tough. "Just part of the life."

I stroked her hair and fixed the pillow gently under her head as I got up. I gestured for Con to keep an eye on her and he nodded. I walked back to the first floor bathroom and stared at myself in the cracked mirror over the sink. I straightened the knot in my tie and smoothed the lapels of my jacket. I splashed some water on my face, spit some blood into the sink, and rubbed my aching stomach. When I came back out Star gestured for me to come to her. I knelt down beside her.

"Do you love me Benny?"

I turned to Con. "she knows more than my Initial."

"Honor student," he replied.

"Don't turn your head away from me boy. Yes or no?"

"You already know."

She turned her face away. "Just like a man."

I leaned over and kissed her gently on the lips. She grimaced a little.

"Sorry."

"It's okay."

"Yes I love you."

"Even after what happened?"

"You didn't do anything wrong Star. God you are so beautiful. Nothing that happened was your fault."

123

She looked at me for a long moment. "I love you too. Now go and get me something."

I went out back to Cole and Junior. Cole was now cutting Junior's hair.

"I have to get Star something."

Cole stayed silent at first. "I said no shit in my house today. You got no respect?"

"I do and I'll respect what you say. But Star's in pain Doc. Look what she's been through. Now Joe's being buried today."

Cole looked off into nowhere. "Sorry, yeah, you're right man. Go up in the attic under the mattress. Take her up there so she can lie down."

A few minutes later Star and I were upstairs and I was holding the flame under the pipe as she took a hit. She offered it to me but I waved it away. She rested her head on my shoulder.

"You know what I'd like?" I asked her.

"What baby?"

"Some time alone with you. Away from all this shit and everyone else so we could just be together."

"That's sweet. Keep it down or the boys'll laugh at you."

"You think we can make that time?"

"I've been played by a lot of guys. You're the only one that ever came through for me. We'll have plenty of time."

Cole, Junior and Con came up the steps and took a seat.

"I hear you two in love," Cole smiled.

I turned to Con. "Rat."

"He was gonna beat it outta me."

Star smiled. "Why we call you Con? How many times was you in prison?"

"Four."

"And you afraid of Doc's punk ass?"

Cole smiled. "Listen, anything you need it's cool okay.

I wasn't thinkin' before."

"She knows you love her. Right babe?"

"Yeah," she grinned. "Big ugly brother loves me."

We all laughed and Cole winked at her.

"Soundin' more like herself every day. Here, gimme some of that."

Star handed the pipe to Cole who loaded a rock and took a hit. He passed it to Junior who did the same, followed by Con and I. Cole opened a bottle of Malt liquor, took a deep slug and passed it around.

"You lock the bottom door?" He asked Con.

"Yeah."

We passed time drinking and smoking and before we knew it the sun had gone down and a lamp lit the room. We had missed Joe's funeral.

"We did it the way he'd like," Cole said.

Junior nodded. "Yeah."

"His Mama might be mad," Con added.

Junior shook his head. "She wouldn't want us there anyway."

Cole nodded. "She don't know."

"Naw."

Cole looked at me. "You real quiet."

"It's nothing."

"Out wit' it."

"I just didn't know him as long as all you guys."

"He was family and so are you. Needy ass nigga."

"You know what I mean."

Cole hid his smile behind the bottle as he drank. "Yeah, cool."

I lit a smoke and handed it to Star, then passed the pack around.

"Taxes is due on the house," Cole said.

"Shit," I answered. "I never thought about that. How much?"

"Fifteen hundred."

"Damn!" Con laughed. "For this roach motel."

"How long do we have?" I asked.

"Six weeks maybe."

"We'll get it."

"Where?" Junior asked.

"We'll take our asses out to work," I announced.

Star laughed and it hurt her mouth. Cole ignored her.

"Doin' what?"

"We'll find something. How long's the house been paid off anyway?"

"My Pop's died ten years ago, so jus' a lil' before that."

Cole caught my eye and nodded in Star's direction. "Tomorrow?"

"Maybe," I answered.

She wasn't supposed to see but did.

"What?"

"Nothing," I told her.

"You better spill it boyfriend."

Cole smirked. "She like your wife. She holdin' the leash an' pullin' your ass along."

Star glared at Cole. "You shut up and you," she turned to me, "talk."

Cole laughed. "She like goin' here doggy, doggy. Doggy."

Junior spit out his beer and Con let out a rare smile. Star flashed me a severe look.

"We need to find the guy who hurt you. We want you to come for a ride and point him out."

Star shook her head. "Enough bad shit already happened. Leave it be."

"So he does it to someone else?"

"Other bitches ain't my concern."

"They're our concern."

"Oh, you the crackhead cops now?"

"We're the only ones who care."

"Your job to care about me an' each other. That's it."

"Oh that's it? Fuck everyone else?"

"Glad you understand."

"I don't."

"I don't want the three of you in jail. Who's gonna stop him from comin' back then?

"Who's gonna stop him now? We can't watch you every second."

"I'll stay close. Beside that we don't know where he live at."

"Only three streets in this town for the nigga's," Cole answered. "This one, one that don't matter, and the one he live on."

Star pointed a finger at him. "No! There's no fuckin' way. You're done wit' it. All of you. I won't point him out so you three end up doin' years in the State. Never, ever."

Cole sat in the front seat beside me and Star sat with Junior in the back. We cruised up and down a fairly rough street checking everyone out. Cole continually pointed to people asking if they were the attacker.

"Him?"

"No," she answered.

"Nigga by the garage?"

"No."

"Over right there?"

"Man, will you please shut the fuck up. I'll tell you when I see him."

"You're not playin' are you?"

"Check yourself nigga. I said I'll do it, I'll do it!"

Cole shrugged and lit two smokes, handing one to me.

"Maybe it's too early," I said."

"Maybe bitch knows we comin'," Cole answered.

"Right on," Junior answered.

I locked eyes with Star in the rear view mirror. "I say we wait," she said.

"You're doin' the right thing," Cole replied.

"No choice wit' you buggin' on me an' your partner up there kissin' on me like a homeless pup...shit!" She slid down on her seat, suddenly panicked.

"Where?" Junior asked.

"By the mailbox," she whispered."

"That big nigga?"

"Yeah."

Cole looked across at the man. "Fuck."

"Holy shit," I said. "Look at the size of him."

"Let's just go!" Star pleaded.

Cole reached back and patted Star's knee. "We gotta hit that boy wit' somethin' big."

"No shit," Junior mumbled.

Cole turned to me. "Take us over B."

"Oh shit Doc."

"Easy now. We okay. Three to one."

"A big fuckin' one," Junior said.

"He's very strong," Star warned.

"He ain't shit," Cole answered. "Now B!"

I pulled the tire iron from under the seat and Cole wrapped his chain around his hand a few times. Junior cracked his knuckles and stretched his neck. I gunned it and pointed the car across the street.

"Here we go!" Cole yelled.

We screeched to halt by the curb, leaving Star alone in the back seat as we jumped out. Cole struck first, smashing the chain into the big man's neck. I hit him hard across the back with the tire iron and Junior began wildly punching him in the face. The man stumbled slightly, took out a blackjack, and smashed it down on top of my head. Searing pain rushed through my skull and I hit the ground hard. Cole kicked him in the groin and wrapped the chain around his neck as he doubled over in pain. Junior pounded him furiously in the head and mid-section. I got to my knees and tossed Junior the tire iron who continued the raging attack. The big man slapped the blackjack across Junior's face, opening up a nasty gash and sending him sprawling to the ground. Cole began to punch him in the face and neck. The big man began swinging back strongly and bloodied Cole's mouth.

I managed to get to my feet though the world seemed to be spinning. I jumped on the man's back and got him in a choke hold. Junior smashed the tire iron up into his groin from the ground as Cole repeatedly smashed his knees with the chain. The big man finally went down with me still on his back. I made sure his face smashed into the concrete then rolled off quickly before he could grab me. The three of us were covered in our own blood as we circled him and began kicking him in the head and torso. I got even dizzier and fell back down to the ground. Cole and Junior continued kicking until they were too exhausted to continue. Cole bent over and put his hands on his knees to catch his breath.

"Nough."

Junior gave him one last kick in the gut. "Spread the word bitch!"

Cole and Junior helped me into the back seat with Star who grabbed me like a lost child. Junior went over to check the big man who was lying motionless on the sidewalk. Cole stood near the car and looked at Star who was crying like a frightened little girl.

"Oh shit man, I think he's dead!" Junior called over to us.

Cole kept looking at us for a moment with a quiet storm building behind his eyes. He walked over to Junior who was still kneeling beside the big man.

"I think he's dead man." Junior repeated.

Cole pulled his gun from behind his back and emptied the clip into the man's head and back. Junior jumped up quickly in shock.

"I know he's dead," Cole said.

Junior grabbed Cole's arm but just stood there frozen

in disbelief.

"Oh shit man! Oh shit!"

He got himself together and pulled Cole toward the car. Cole stopped for one last look.

"My lil' sister."

Junior shoved him into the front seat of the car then ran around to the driver's side. He jumped in and hit the gas.

We never spoke of it again. Not in the car or the house, never. When a person as beautiful as Star is hurt like that everybody who knows her suffers as well.Maybe we couldn't kill off all of our pain, but we could fuckin' kill him. For the moment, that was enough.

Cole, Junior and I sat side by side on a hospital cot while Star slouched in a chair across from us. Doctor Durham entered the room and looked us up and down.

He turned his gaze on Cole.

"I see you found him."

"Naw. Tripped over a damn dog."

"All three of you?"

"Their sorry asses always following right behind me."

The Doctor turned to Star. "Your homies out defending your honor?"

"Nobody use that word homie no more Doc."

"Was that a yes?"

"No. They tripped over a grungy ass dog."

The Doctor sighed. "Are you feeling okay?"

"Yes Sir."

"Better now I'm guessing."

"Yes Sir."

"Helluva life kids."

"Yes Sir," Star and I replied in unison.

The Doctor consulted his charts for a moment then looked at me. "You have a slight concussion. I'll give you some pain meds . Count on headaches for up to a year."

He turned to Junior. "The stitches will come out on their own but change the bandage at least once a day. I'll give you some to take home."

He turned to Cole. "Mister Coleman, you lost a couple of teeth and split your gum. Go see a Dentist and get checked out. I'll give you a couple days worth of pain meds as well."

"Thanks Doc," I said.

"You're welcome boys." He turned to Star. "It's a fine line between love and insanity."

She pointed to Cole and I. "Those two love me, Junior jus' showin' off."

"I see," The Doctor smiled.

"Thanks for lookin' out Doc," she added.

"Yes, well, being as none of you have medical

insurance I'm going to pretend like you were never here. Unless of course the police come and ask me."

"Police don't care about no damn dog," Star answered.

The Doctor couldn't help but smile. "Yes, I suppose that's true."

A few days later Star and I were carrying the last few items of value that I owned out of my apartment to bring to the pawn shop. Soon we were right back smoking crack in the attic and watching Cole search through an over-filled ashtray for a butt that he could still light. Star began searching the floor for a rock that may have but most likely didn't drop. I coughed out a little blood and spit it out in the trash can. I took a deep chug of cheap liquor and flinched at the burning.

Ever feel like your life is out of control? Like you're

doing a downward spiral into the darkness headed for a place you can never come back from? The party turns into addiction in an instant. Just like love. One moment you're fine and the next you're completely destroyed. There's no more party, just the mission. Get what you need at all costs....All costs.

Chapter Four: The End

Two months had passed since Star had been attacked. Her face looked empty and hollow and mine sickly and gray. I picked up an envelope someone had slid under my apartment door and handed it to Star who opened it.

"Dear Mister, blah, blah, ...Three months since you paid any rent blah, blah, ...Please vacate the premises immediately to avoid eviction by the Sheriff's department."

I fell down onto the bed and surveyed the room. "The furniture's pretty nice. I bet we could get a few buck's for it."

Star smiled happily. "And smoke it up in one night."

"Fuckin' right."

"I know a guy who'll give us a deal."

"We're never here anyway."

"Fuck this asshole."

"Yeah."

She jumped on the bed and straddled me.

"Crazy woman."

"This is fun." she said. "You get it now don't you?"

"Get what?"

"The lifestyle. Living from moment to moment. The freedom."

"Yeah well, I took a good crack to the head."

She punched me lightly. "You know you get it."

"I got poisoned too with some drain cleaner or somethin'."

"Quit exaggerating."

"Maybe it was all that."

"Maybe," she smiled, "It was me."

I paused and looked at her. "No."

She hit me again playfully. "I love you."

"You still wanna hang with a homeless guy."

"You can stay at Doc's. You and me."

"I didn't ask where I'd stay."

"I'm with you ain't I?"

I pulled her down and rested her head on my shoulder.

"We'll get this stuff sold off today and leave in the morning. We got anything left?"

"Sure baby."

Star went to get her bag from the table and pulled out a tiny bag and needle. I got up and tied a rubber strap around my arm as she prepared the shot. I looked around the place once again. Most everything was gone. It was bare and empty. Very much like myself I thought.

Cole sat on the living room safa, looking at his own reflection in the picture window. He looked ten years older and sickly as he drank from a cheap bottle of wine. Junior was sitting on the wall just outside keeping watch as usual. Cole watched his lifelong friend for a few minutes and enjoyed the peaceful quiet. It was cut short by the sudden flashing of red lights down the block. They became closer and closer. Junior stood up suddenly and turned to look at Cole. His face was frozen with panic.

Cole jumped up and dropped the bottle. It had no sooner hit the floor when the police vehicles were screeching to a halt in front of his house. He headed for the stairs as officers tackled Junior on the front lawn. Others rushed from a van and headed for Cole's front door. He ran up the steps three at a time as fast as he could. He slammed the lower door closed and threw the heavy bolt over before heading up the rest of the way to the attic. He reached the top and began to frantically gather up needles, crack pipes and empty vials. He grabbed his gun from under a pillow and felt for the empty spot above a ceiling beam. The attic door burst open as he tried to hide the gun. He was too late. Three officers ran up with weapons pointed at him.

"DROP IT NOW!"

Cole dropped the gun and the officers rushed him, shoving him down to the floor. He cringed as they snapped the cuffs tightly on his wrists.

It was dark when my phone rang. I answered half asleep.

"Hello?...What?... Oh fuck no!"

I turned on the lamp, jumped up and began walking in small circles as I talked.

Star sat up and rubbed her eyes.

"When?" I asked. "Fuck! Fuck! Alright, call me back."

My hands were trembling as I hung up.

"That was Con. Cole's house got raided. Cops took him and Junior."

Star looked as if something had just sucked the life right out of her. "Oh my God. Oh my God B! What should we do?"

"He had a couple grams and a shitload of other crap. The worse thing is they found the gun. Con's gonna see if the judge is setting bail."

"But we don't have any money."

"We'll steal some."

"It'll be alright."

"Yeah, alright."

The next morning she and I were sitting on Cole's sofa wearing the same clothes as the day before. Con sat in Cole's easy chair looking defeated. The place had been absolutely trashed by the cops. Con shifted uneasily.

"Judge told me that if I get involved they're sending my ass back up for good."

"He mention bail?" I asked.

"He say Junior violated and goin' straight for a two year jus' for bein' here. He say second time for Doc an' he had a gun. He doin' at least five man. No bail. No money anyway man."

I rubbed my temples. "Doctor was right about the headaches."

"Cops say i can clean up," Con said. "Then I gotta stay out or they lock my ass up wit' 'em."

"Just leave it man. They'll grab you next. Stay away for a few weeks and outta sight."

Con and I stood up and embraced. "It's been real bro," he told me. He turned to Star. "See you round baby-doll."

"Peace," Star smiled at him through her tears. He bent down to hug her and then was out the door.

"I'm scared," she said.

"Me too."

"Where we go now?"

"I don't know but we can't stay here. Demond's gonna know we're alone. You have any clothes here?"

"Yeah, not much."

"Throw them in a bag and let's go."

On a dark street full of factories and warehouses we sat in the car passing the crack pipe back and forth. The car was stuffed with our clothes and a few personal items from my place and Cole's. I looked at her and she smiled back at me.

"This is the end."

"No."

"It is Star. There's nothing left we can do."

She trembled as she took another hit then tried to smile again. "You're too uptight. It's just the stress of this shit."

I stared off into the darkness. "I really do love you."

"What is it with you and bein' in the car that you get so serious?"

"For one thing, I live in it now."

"Place need's a woman's touch," she trembled violently for a moment then pulled herself back together. "Good that I came."

I took her hand. "We have to get out baby. There are no moves left to make. Please. Let's just check into a rehab or something."

"Yeah right. Where'd that come from?"

"You and me. We'll go together."

"Can I bring my pipe?"

"Come on. I'm serious."

"I'm not going. You want to, you can go. I got a couple

of cousins I can crash with."

"What I'm saying is, I don't wanna lose you."

"You don't have to. Go do your fuckin' rehab and pick me up when you get out."

"You'll be alone."

"I'll be cool."

We sat in silence for a long time. If you do enough drugs you can kill off your emotions completely. You feel nothing. But in that moment she broke my heart. She was like a prisoner who'd been in too long. Afraid of the real world. My eyes grew watery.

"I just can't take this shit anymore. Look at me. I'm fuckin' dirty all the time, always fucked up. Always running some dumb ass mission. I can't even pay the rent and take care of you."

Star looked out the window. "If it works on you then I'll go."

"Really?"

She ruffled my hair. "Yes, really."

She leaned over and kissed my cheek. "You'll get a good job when you get out baby and we'll get a new place and order Chinese and watch movies and shit. And we'll make love the day you come home. I'll be waiting for you."

She turned back to look out her window, not wanting me to see her cry.

"Drive me to my cousins now. And by the way," she turned back to me, "I love you too. We'll make this work."

I kissed her, started the car, then paused. "I know it's kinda stupid, but if I had any money I'd give you something. A ring or something you know?"

She took my hand and smiled.

"But I have this chain, with a Saint Christopher medal, he protects you from harm. I took it from around my neck and placed it around hers. She clutched it to her and began to cry harder.

"We'll be fine baby. I promise."

"Yeah, she said. We'll be fine."

Cole and I sat facing each other through the glass in the visitor room, speaking on the wall phones. Cole was dressed in a bright orange County jumpsuit.

"Look at this shit here man," he complained. "I'm gonna be one a them nigga's pickin'up trash along the highway."

"Better than your own clothes. More in fashion."

"Shit. Clothes don't make this man."

"Sorry about everything man."

"Ain't so bad. Food better'n at home. Carrots an'potatoes an' some shit I dunno what it is."

We laughed.

"Okay, not so loud. Bitches'll hit me wit' the stick."

"When's your trial?"

"Dunno. Free lawyer don't call me."

"Junior's away for two."

"Yeah, I saw him 'fore he transferred out."

"Sorry about your house. They fucked it all up."

"Taxes been due anyway. They gonna take it anyhow."

"Oh shit man. You'll lose the house?"

"Ain't nobody gonna buy that piece a shit."

I laughed. "True."

"You been doin' somethin' useful wit' that girl?"

"Of course."

"Pleae nigga, You can't lie for shit. You ain't done nutin' worthwhile wit' her. You the dumbest ass nigger I keep swearin' it. Get your head all bust open an' shit for her an' can't even get some. Sweet Jesus in heaven what's wrong wit' your mind boy?"

I laughed. "Hey, you need anything?"

"You ain't got nuthin'."

"I'm going into rehab man."

"Mmm, hmm."

"Star says if it works for me she'll go."

"Believe it when I see it brother. Where she at now?"

"At her cousins."

He rubbed his chin. "Well, they sorry ass crackheads but they'll look out."

"I'll come see you."

Cole leaned forward, inches from the glass. He looked into my eyes.

"You stay away now man. Don't come up there to the State. You gonna do this then do it right. Otherwise shit was for nuthin'."

"What're you saying?"

"I'm sayin' save yourself bro. This shit in here another world. I can't look out for you if you end up in here man.

154

And you can't look out for her."

"What's that got to do with visiting you?"

"You wanna help me man, stay away. Ease my mind. I don't need to be worryin' 'bout you two. Go do somethin' usefull wit' that girl for sweet heaven's sake."

"I'll see you when you get out."

"Much love man."

Cole hung up, then me. We looked at each other a moment, both emotional but holding it back. Cole made a peace sign and I did the same. Then he was gone. The police soon made Cole's gun as the one used in the murder of the big man. He was charged and convicted of second degree murder. Before sentencing the judge asked him if he felt any remorse. He rubbed his chin in thought for a moment then answered, "Fuck no."

He got life.

I sat in a circle with eight other residents and a Counselor named Charmaine. They all came from different walks of life, some street addicts, some white collar weekend warriors. Some were young and some were old. Charmaine was very direct. Unless shit started getting really nasty she let us all just have at it and tear each other up. No one knows a liar like another liar. There's a lot of bullshit in rehab. You dish it out and you listen to it non-stop. When you're all out of bullshit you get to leave. It takes quite a while.

"You're holding out Karen. You're not fooling anyone but yourself."

Karen sat silently looking at her folded hands in her lap. Charmaine shook her head.

"How about you Benny?"

"I feel good. I get a lot of urges but I feel good."

"You thinking of any plans for the future?"

I smiled. "One or two."

She looked suspicious. "Mmm. We'll find out what's behind that smirk later. For now I want to do a little exercise. I'm going to place two chairs in the center of the circle. On one chair I'm going to place an empty white box. I want you to pretend that your drug of choice is inside that box. One at a time you will come up and face it and say your goodbyes."

Star sat alone in a dark corner. She was shaking terribly and being ignored by the other eight or so addicts in the large room. A man was passed out with a needle in his arm, another had pissed his pants, one vomited in the opposite corner while others took hits of crack from makeshift beer can pipes. Star lifted the needle to her arm and blasted the heroin into her vein. Her eyes instantly glazed over and her mouth dropped open. She tried to get up but went right back down on her knees. A couple of people nearby pointed at her and laughed. They sounded hollow and distant. Tears ran down her face as she pulled the needle out of her arm. She reached around her neck and took off the medal Benny had given her. She looked at it a moment then clutched her fist around it tightly.

The chairs were set up for the exercise. Charmaine asked If I would like to volunteer and go first. I sat in the center chair and flashed a grin at the group. I looked down at the tiny white box and my grin faded away. I suddenly felt very troubled. Like I was about to say goodbye to all I had left in the world. I know that it's supposed to be emotionally crippling but I swear that the time I'd spent on the street saved my life. How do we ever know if it's our things that make us happy and not the lives we're living? Our large screen televisions and computers and fucking rotating pizza ovens and all that other useless shit. I caught myself daydreaming and looked up at the group. They were waiting patiently.

"We've been together a long time," I began. "I guess I want to say I've learned from you. I've also been destroyed because of you. The darkest day of my life was the day I met you. But...You're also responsible for the very brightest day."

Star lay dead on the dirty floor with wide open eyes and white vomit running from her mouth. Her hand was open, the Saint Christopher medal laying inches from her fingers. Forever out of reach. A car screeched to a halt outside and Doctor Durham made his way inside to meet Con who'd frantically called him. The Doctor knelt down beside her and checked her pulse without needing to. Tears fell from his cheeks."

"Sweet Lord. Just a beautiful baby."

Con stared at Star in absolute disbelief. Doctor Durham looked up at him. "How many more do we need to see like this before it's over son?"

"Goodbye," I finished and wiped the tears from my face. An emptiness came upon me like I'd never felt in my life and I moved numbly back to my seat. It wasn't till a week later that I dropped some coins into the payphone and called Con.

"Who dat?" he answered.

"It's me man."

"Yo. What up B? Good to hear you man. How's it going?"

"It's going alright. You?"

"You know man. Wit' all that's going on."

"You hear from Doc?"

"Yeah man. He say he's glad you stayed in there wit' all that happened wit' Star an' all."

"What do you mean with Star?"

He was silent for a few seconds. "Oh shit B. You don't know?"

"What man? She's okay right?"

Con bent over his kitchen counter, his head in his hands. "B, man."

"What the fuck man! Yes or no?"

"I'm sorry. She gone Bro."

"She left? For where?"

"She's dead man. Overdose."

I couldn't speak. Con held on with me silently.

"Was...was she alone?"

"I don't know man....I'm sorry brother."

I beat the receiver against the phone , first slowly then harder and violently.

"No,no,no,no,no!"

I dropped the phone and fell to my knees sobbing. Charmaine came running and bent down to hold me. In that moment I felt as empty as I possibly could. As completely empty as any man could ever be.

I brushed out my cigarette and continued to watch Demond conduct his business down the street. A car pulled up to the curb in front of me and Doctor Durham climbed out.

He walked up the lawn and took a seat beside me on the front stoop.

"An interesting place to meet considering all those we might have chosen."

"You said the city was ugly for you now but you remember it as beautiful. It's like that for me right here, now. I wanted to show you."

I lit two smokes and instinctively handed one to him. He took it without comment.

"It'll be hard to leave here," I said.

He looked around for a moment at the littered streets and cracked sidewalks.

"For a while young friend, but soon the pain will ease just a little bit and then one day a little more until maybe someday it too will become just a memory."

"Has your pain become a memory?"

He smiled and shook his head slowly. "No."

We sat together silently for a while, him smoking his pipe and me smoking my cheap cigarettes. He put his arm around my shoulder.

"One day a beautiful young family will laugh and love and dream in this big home Benny. All because you and Mister Coleman left it behind."

"You think so?"

"That will be my hope."

I looked up at the boarded attic window and smiled.

"Yeah, mine too."